# BOCA GRANDE

*by Loren Singer*

BOCA GRANDE

THAT'S THE HOUSE, THERE

THE PARALLAX VIEW

*LOREN SINGER*

# BOCA GRANDE

*Doubleday & Company, Inc., Garden City, New York*
*1974*

*Library of Congress Cataloging in Publication Data*

Singer, Loren.
Boca Grande. 
I. Title.
PZ4.S6178Bo [PS3569.I545] 813'.5'4

ISBN: 0-385-05521-8
LIBRARY OF CONGRESS CATALOG CARD NUMBER 73-20531

PRINTED IN THE UNITED STATES OF AMERICA
FIRST EDITION

For their assistance with the technical
aspects of this book I am grateful to
Frederic C. Kapp
Lawrence A. Rosenstadt

The Brotherhood is not by the blood certainly:
But neither are men brothers by speech—by saying so:
Men are brothers by life lived . . .

ARCHIBALD MAC LEISH
"Speech to Those Who Say Comrade"

# BOCA GRANDE

"Expect them, Brothers, they will come. By sea, by air. But all their might avails them nothing. We will resist them. We shall never give in."
BOCA GRANDE 8 / 28

The sun rose slowly, a distinct white circle in the mist of the August morning, and brightened the bow and the lower rigging. Lovell woke. To port, a dinghy worked its way out from a nearby cove. It was rowed with delicacy across the still water, the oars rising and falling in quiet rhythm.

It altered course and disappeared under the stern of *Avatar*. There was a bump of rub rail at starboard. Lovell recognized two of them, the small one at the oars and the man in the bow who rose gingerly, painter in hand, to make the dinghy fast.

Perkinson and Amat.

Perkinson shook his hand heartily through the lifelines. Lovell released the pelican hook, and as Amat scrambled aboard, the third man in the stern edged forward.

Perkinson executed an unmilitary salute and climbed up.

"Permission to come aboard, sir," he said, smiling.

"Granted," Lovell replied and sat up in his sleeping bag.

The third man boarded, and Amat introduced them.

"Bailey Madden," he said in his slightly accented English, and gestured at Lovell. "Captain Lovell, Bailey, John Lovell."

Madden shook his hand, once, and nodded.

Perkinson breathed deeply and smote his chest.

"Nothing like a sea voyage, however short," he said and, glancing at the cabin hatch, nodded in question.

Lovell tossed the sleeping bag across the boom.

"Didn't you know I was alone, Perk?" he said.

"He's never certain," Madden said. "Not one hundred per cent certain."

Lovell pushed the hatch cover back and dropped down into the cabin, picked up his dungarees, and dressed quickly.

"I was pretty certain," Perkinson said equably. "Would you have a cup of coffee on board?"

"And scrambled eggs and bacon for four. You for bacon, Mat?"

Amat nodded, somewhat ruefully. "So ended my Mohammedanism. Now I eat pork sausages, pork chops, and when I have a sandwich at my desk, it is ham."

Lovell filled the big enamelware pot and set it on the stove. He pumped up the alcohol pressure, opened the burner to prime it, and lit the reservoir. He watched the flame.

"How long have you been watching me, Perk?" he asked, measuring coffee into the pot.

Perkinson sat down on the settee across the cabin from him.

"Oh, three or four days, I imagine." He smiled again as Lovell moved about the galley, slicing bacon professionally, cutting bread from a day-old loaf. "We saw the rest leave last night. You make a fine short-order cook."

It pleased Lovell that he had noticed it. It was a part of Perkinson, a reserved, unerring appreciation of another's abilities, simple approbation, casual yet particular, that generated reciprocal good will, co-operation, eventually devotion.

Perkinson's remark covered much: the painstakingly sharpened cook's knife, the scoured cutting board, the airy cabin, brightwork gleaming in the summer morning, the polished brass of the compass mount, the clean chrome-plated cleats.

Lovell glowed. Over the years he had accomplished much and Perkinson was saying so with the pleasing indirectness that cements relationships for a lifetime.

He turned the bacon again to crisp it properly, drained the excess fat, broke eight eggs into the big skillet, and stirred them gently. While he waited, he poured coffee and passed cups to Amat and Madden in the cockpit.

"Well," said Perkinson, raising his cup, "better days."

Lovell nodded and sipped.

They ate, companionably, in the cockpit. Off to port there was a sudden riffle on the still water.

"What kind of fish?" Amat asked.

"Spearing, they call them," Lovell answered. "The snappers, small blue fish, are chasing them. That's the food chain. Just below the surface you'll see flashes of silver. They turn on their sides and snap."

"Good eating?" Madden asked indifferently.

Lovell lit a cigarette. He grinned.

"There's a difference of opinion." He settled himself comfortably back against the cushions in the stern.

"Some people in the harbor eat the spearing. They take them in square nets that they stretch with hanger wire, you see, about three feet square. You drop your net in the water about eighteen inches below the surface and chum over it—sprinkle cat food or canned mackerel or something."

Madden grimaced in distaste.

Lovell nodded.

"To each his own. If you take that attitude, flounders are

even worse. A flounder is on the bottom, flapping his way along in all that shit, and winds up in a restaurant as 'Filet of Sole Bonne Femme.' That would be six and a half dollars, table d'hôte. But the flesh is beautiful, white, firm. Very good."

Amat was rolling a cigarette, the little white bag of tobacco held in his mouth by its yellow string.

"Your friend from Runge, Texas," Lovell said. Amat nodded and mumbled.

"Mulbarger, or Clawhammer, was his name."

"Kittsmiller," Perkinson said.

Amat tucked the bag back in the pocket of his shirt. It was, Lovell thought, a rare sort of personal trace element, not only a response to a man but to a civilization. It was Amat's commitment. When he smoked, he smoked as a Texan from the Panhandle.

"That's Manhattan down there, isn't it?" Madden said. He spoke with a definite sense of time, even here in the still anchorage on this quiet morning, turning the conversation away from the past, away from shared experience, back to now.

"That is Manhattan," Lovell agreed. "And to your left is Long Island. That shore is what they used to call the Gold Coast. Maybe they still do. But it isn't really. It's a mass of flat-roofed, one-story houses, more and more parking lots and concrete plazas that reflect so much heat in summer that the ocean breezes rise way the hell up in the air and pass right over the Sound. In August the prevailing wind here is the overshot southerly.

"And behind me is—after a hundred sea miles or so—Block Island, and after that England via the great circle route. You turn right—starboard that is—and you hit Florida eventually. Right?"

Madden looked at him dispassionately. He rose and stretched out, enormously.

"Thanks," he said. "Now I'm oriented."

Lovell turned to Perkinson. The mist on the black water was dissolving now, shredding away from the mooring area, lying only in patches close upon the surface.

"What are you doing here, Perk?" he said. "Great to see you but I don't think it was because you missed me, was it?"

Perkinson took a small portable recorder from his jacket pocket, set it on a seat, and turned it on.

In Spanish a voice exhorted, sobbed, whispered in hoarse passion, sounded a martial call, wailed a plea. Lovell covered his ears in pain.

"Let me translate," Perkinson said, and spun the tape ahead. Now the voice was English, flat and with a midwestern twang to it, and it delivered the locution as though calling livestock prices on the Chicago exchange.

"And still they come, Brothers! Still they come. No longer with their weapons to overwhelm us with steel. We showed them throughout our glorious past how much of our blood we could shed in defense of our beloved shore–and how much of theirs. They can take our land from us, but not while there is a rock left to build our last defense, not while there is a single patriot with enough strength remaining to resist.

"Now they come with their ideas. They offer peace and friendship. But we know better. They will give us the grinding heel of the master to place upon our necks. They will take our sons to enslave and our daughters to revile and our land to despoil."

"It loses something in the translation," Perkinson told him wryly, snapping off the little machine. "But you can see that it comes on pretty strong. And it goes on for eighteen hours a day."

"They have a lot of lung power," Madden said. "That's one area where they're second to nobody. They learned from the best."

"They're distributing, they've been distributing thousands of single-frequency receivers, cheap little gimmicks, all over the whole area." Amat smiled. "Made in Hong Kong, or maybe Jeua. People's Receiver Model 1950."

"Maybe right in my old home kampong."

"That," said Perkinson, "is a radio transmitter called Boca Grande locally.

"When I say locally, I mean that it has an enormous range, larger than anything else in the Caribbean. We don't know how much actual influence it has—"

Madden interrupted him.

"It's got the same influence that our own have. These are much less sophisticated people. They listen to that garbage long enough, and it has an effect. An effect that could lose us a whole continent. Half a world. Not just in terms of markets, but in people who are going to be our deadly enemies."

Lovell poured a cup of coffee and offered the pot around. Particularly to Madden, who gestured it away impatiently.

"One political lecture at a time is plenty," he said, idly.

"What do you want of me?"

"I'm not sure," said Perkinson, turning his cup this way and that. "My great-aunt used to be able to read fortunes in coffee grounds. Much more difficult than teacups. She always said that I would be a very complicated man with a complicated work. Probably because my father owned a woolen mill, and she knew he wanted me to come into it. Not a cup did she turn upside down and have me tap the bottom three times that didn't have all sorts of lines running around it. Skeins and bobbins, bobbins and skeins.

"Well," he said, pursing his lips, "we have to interrupt these mouthings, at a particular time, for a particular time, and with no political complications."

"It should be sown with salt," Madden said.

"That is, we may have to," Perkinson amended. "It can't be definite until, oh, right up to the last minute, say."

"Somebody ought to have the guts to make the decision right now," Madden said abruptly. "Make it and stick by it."

Perkinson ignored him. It was not, Lovell remembered, his style to sit on anyone. He counseled with himself and with as many other viewpoints as he could find that differed, collecting methodically, examining, weighing, and finally deciding. There was room for every shade of opinion and understanding, if it occurred or could be stated to him.

"We have to be flexible because a very important trip will be made into Boca Grande's territory sometime next year. Sometime between March and April is all we know at the moment, and when the trip is made it should have some sort of atmosphere of good will, or at least objectivity. Not such a much of rage and threat and passion.

"So we think it would be a good thing if we could interrupt these transmissions for two or three days before, maybe five or six days all told.

"Then the people in the area could hear what our man is going to say and offer and what our thinking is. We'd use their frequency."

"For the sake of sweet reason," said Lovell smiling, "you want to cut Boca Grande's throat."

"No," said Perkinson, "we want to pinch its windpipe."

Madden stared in disgust at the skyline over the bow. Amat listened impassively. He cleared his throat and spoke.

"It's a gentler imperialism than ever before. As such things go, it's a gesture, and very significant, I think."

"I'm not so sure," Lovell told him. "It's patronizing, for one thing. I would think that you'd be more aware of that than anybody else, Amat."

Lovell could read nothing in his expression, or in his eyes. No hint that Amat bin Suleiman knew the downtrodden of this world better than Samuel Paine Perkinson or John Lovell or Bailey Madden.

Lovell remembered him speaking about it one night. About how he had come to this strange career of his, how he had suddenly understood that what he knew and what he was could transform him into a man of the West, a contributor of knowledge and understanding in an area that encompassed a whole world.

"I had jumped my ship," Mat had told him, "in Los Angeles—below Los Angeles. It was a Dutch freighter, and we brought ore to the West Coast. I was sixteen years old and I had been working on ships already since I was fourteen. There was a system of payment then. All classified—on shore too.

"A Chinese would work for less than a Malay—a Chinese would work for less than anybody, except a Korean. A half-caste might make more—if he had blue eyes. A Filipino for a very little more.

"By more, I mean the part of a guilder a month. But the ships took you to the ocean, which was clean, cleaner than the towns, or where we lived in the towns. Not near the boulevards, not even near enough for the winds to take the smells from our houses into the embassies and the consulates.

"The ship was the *Oryx* out of Rotterdam. Years later when I read *Lord Jim* I recognized that ship at once. *Oryx* was bigger, and the captain more courageous.

"But I knew nothing of the size of the Pacific. To me it was another world. It was measured in days. Two days from Singapore to Batavia. Three days to Ceylon. Twenty days to Kobe. To Marika, fifty-five days.

"So when we arrived and after we had unloaded and were waiting for a cargo to be found, the mate gave a few of us each a ten dollar bill—he marked it down in his book. He printed the name of the ship on a piece of paper, and the pier number, and the time to be back, and he told us that the Americans would arrest us and put us in prison and our fathers would never see us again if we did not come back."

He had taken from his handsome wallet a piece of paper torn from a pocket notebook, had unfolded it carefully and had handed it to Lovell.

"'S.S. *Oryx*,' it read, 'Pier Sixty-three, Port Los Angeles.'"

Amat had grinned widely.

"That is the first entry in my personal file. Before that I had no file.

"So I went ashore. To this day, when I am in a port city I go to the docks to walk up and down and watch the sailors and the stevedores. I look in the windows of the stores that face the waterfront. Work clothes at unknown prices. Green suits made of very hard material that doesn't wear very well. The only city I know that has good clothes for sailors is Venice. Perhaps because they have been in business for six centuries.

"I had left the ship with another Malay. He was a man of the world and would go directly to a whorehouse. He wanted me to come with him, but that meant nothing to me. He said there were fine girls here, from Hollywood, and they screwed like the Javanese, soft and pleasant that is, like an ocean wave. But I didn't go, so he told me how much money this ten dollars was in guilders and in Straits dollars and in pounds. I was very confused.

"So we parted at the gate to the wharf and a trolley car came along—there was a trolley car that ran from Los Angeles all the way out to the shore towns.

"My shipmate had placed me so, to get the car going into the town. One came and I got on and gave the operator my ten dollars. He got very angry at me. Worse than if I had tried to cheat him, I imagine. He wouldn't change my note and I had to get off.

"It's curious that this happened. I then thought that I should go back to the ship, you see, but then as I was making up my mind another trolley car came along in the opposite direction and I tried again. I got on and this man gave me change for my note, probably because he was coming to the end of his run, and I got off at a very pretty little town called Newport Beach and I walked down to the water where there were many sailboats tied up. Some were small but some were very large. Yachts. I walked along past them. No one bothered me, and in one there was a man sitting in the stern drinking beer from a bottle, you see.

"He looked familiar to me. Different somehow, and yet familiar. With a big, red glowing face.

"He called out to me. 'Hey,' he said. 'Hey you! You want job? Catchee job workee for me?'

"I took the job. Sixty dollars a month. Houseboy, butler, steward, everything. He was a cowboy star. Very big with women and whiskey, but a very kind man. He read a lot too. That's where I stayed for two years until the war came.

"From there to the language school at the Presidio. First I was an informant, but I had more knowledge than most of the informants. They had never lived here, never lived on the terms I had with Ralph. Ralph Bennett was his name.

"They had two problems with teaching that I did not have. They had no vocabulary to speak of in either Malay or in English. Theoretically, that is not bad for an informant, but it is not good either."

His voice faded, the soft gentle voice that had gone on with tolerant amusement at a particular difficulty as he had made his way further along in this complex, uncaring society that had begun its relationship with the man by using him, and then finding itself used by him, as he moved sometimes laterally toward some unconsidered goal, knowing that it was there.

Now he had no more knowledge of the peasant than either of them. There was a difference between an Indonesian slum a quarter century ago and the movements that surged through a nation today. Amat was an anachronism as dated as he was.

Lovell glanced seaward. Suddenly he was angry at them.

They had brought years with them. Alone on *Avatar*, he could be any age that he wished and any man that he wished. He need not suffer the awareness of the time that had passed, and of their impress on his mind, and frighteningly sometimes on his body. So much the same as any other but so different, because it was his own. That sacred, self-sufficient cosmic temple. Rather a comic temple, with a Renaissance front, a Baroque entry, and an unreinforced concrete shell made in America.

"So, Perk," he said, "us old shipmates will hop on board *Avatar*, lay on a big supply of gin and cocktail frankfurters, and go and pinch Boca Grande's windpipe."

"It's crossed my mind," Perkinson admitted.

"About a twenty-three-hundred-mile voyage. If we went down the inland waterway that would take about two weeks, unless we sailed at night too. But that would mean running aground ten or fifteen times and having to be pulled off, or busting our behinds pulling ourselves off."

"But I do get to be captain, right?"

"Nobody else is equipped for the job."

"The last five or six hundred miles would be open ocean. And you would want to pinpoint your landfall."

"I'm qualified," Bailey Madden said flatly.

"How qualified?" Lovell asked. "Suppose you couldn't get a sun or star sight for two days or three."

"That would be my responsibility, not yours." He had the manner of vintage army officer addressing an AWOL room orderly.

"What would your cover be?" Lovell said. He turned away from Madden deliberately. "It's certainly a patrolled coast, and you would have to come in to within three or four hundred yards of the shore. That's without seeing a chart. I imagine you three have been looking at recent ones."

Amat nodded.

"We have picked a place, subject to revision of course. But

it's a gradual shoal beginning about a thousand yards offshore—you have still beyond that point about ten feet at low water until about four hundred yards off the beach."

Perkinson sucked on a cold pipe.

"The cover is the reason we're here," he said. There was no longer the bantering tone he had spoken in previously. Now it was business.

"There is a yacht race every other year. It leaves from Nassau, goes through the Windward Passage, and winds up in Jamaica."

Lovell nodded.

"Right. I understand it's a very interesting kind of race. It's more of a challenge than most—lots of course changes, you have to pick your way from island to island, you've got to be careful of the currents, and, of course, it's very beautiful. Lovely area, and the winds are fairly consistent at that time of the year."

"The Northeast Trades."

"Set your watch by them."

"Your correspondent at Guantanamo?"

Perkinson shook his head impatiently.

"We can discuss that, and we will. Let's keep our attention on the cover for the moment. It's suited to our plan. It's properly flexible. It's feasible. Would you like to go?"

From the moment that they had come aboard Lovell had savored this time, this point at which they would offer him some great boon. It would be nothing for them to offer it, and they would have no realization of how much he wanted it, and what he would do for it. Nor could he tell them what this hint of freedom meant to him. It was like a chink of blue sky penetrating to a cellar, a dancing beam of sunlight, the motes winking as he watched.

There was a tiny smile on Bailey Madden's face and Lovell knew how much his own expression had revealed. He could make some attempt to wrap himself once more in the calm, pleasant but disinterested attitude that was his presence to almost everyone about him. It would not be accepted by these three.

"What boat would you use?" He temporized.

Perkinson shrugged.

"What's wrong with this one?"

Lovell did not answer him immediately. He took from the lazaret at his feet the little flag that he used as a private signal. It was a copy of "Don't Tread on Me." His son had given it to him on Father's Day. Over the years he had exclaimed as enthusiastically as a man of his disposition might over the matched sets of shaving lotion, the sailing shirts, and the ties that showed up with such unmulled constancy, but the pennant indicated more—perhaps a more accurate understanding of the fixture that was he.

He hooked it to the halliard and raised it rapidly and smoothly to *Avatar*'s masthead, hitched it smartly to its cleat, and sat down upon the cabin top.

"It doesn't make any sense to take this boat in the shape she's in. I can't now and never have been able to afford the kind of gear and conditioning that would make it competitive. That's a rich man's race and I'm just barely able to keep her as is—afloat."

He looked at Perkinson with directness.

"I'm not a yachtsman, I'm an amateur shipwright, painter, rigger, mechanic. I maintain my position in the society by clinging with my nails. I put up a front. I pretend independence."

"Don't you have it?" Perkinson asked. "I thought you did."

"I did. Not so much any more. Advancing age. If you make a commitment to a society like this one you have to maintain it, strengthen it, believe in it, like a Crusader."

"A sad life," said Madden, stretching. "Young Scotch and old yachts."

"What did you bring him for," Lovell said, "to balance the dinghy?"

"Truly," Perkinson said with utter falsity, "I thought you'd like each other. He reminds me a little of you, Lovell, when you were younger."

"Not so much humor, though," Amat said, smiling. "Bailey is a serious man with a serious job and a serious purpose."

"You know," Madden said, "I'm not trying to annoy you, any of you. But we can't be successful in what we're attempting unless one of us is willing to be direct.

"The three of you belong to another time. You had some sense of idealism about your comradeship, you helped each other through the tough parts, you shared.

"You were among the first to admit Amat here to—what? Equal rights, privileges. Maybe you even broke the color line in a Washington restaurant with him.

"But the best days are all back of you. Maybe you still have this idealism. Maybe you're still good comrades and friends. I doubt it.

"From listening to you talk—not you, of course, Lovell—and watching your behavior, Perk, I don't think you believe in what you're doing any longer. I don't think it has much meaning to you. I think you're more concerned about old age and the usefulness of your last twenty years.

"You won't grant me any kind of sincerity for behaving the way you did in *my* time. You think I'm not only not as smart, but pretty damn dumb.

"Don't you?"

Interested, Lovell nodded.

"Well, I think you were. I think your war was fought at the wrong time with the wrong people, that too much was spent on it in people and materiel, that it was misleading to the

American people, and that the problems victory brought are more of a threat than the ones you solved.

"What is really worse about you is that you argue about my commitment. I'm the one who has the vitality and the energy and the desire to maintain my position. But now all you slaughterers are feeling sorry for the animals."

He spat over the side.

"I don't think this is much of an operation. I don't think it's worth the complexities you've brought up so far, and God help me, the ones you'll bring up in the future. You all lost the motivations that people have to have to survive.

"I don't want to be associated with you, but I went along and came here, hoping that maybe you, Lovell, would just possibly be some kind of throwback. But Christ, you're just like these two. One wants to be the first coloured with a 'u' to head a desk in Washington and the other wants to teach the dynamics of Geopolitik at Georgetown."

Perkinson's face flamed a fiery red. Mat wrapped himself in dark impassiveness. They were demeaned together.

"Together we work for a bright future for all of us, each in his own way to the best of his ability. We need no whips to urge us on, only the greatness of Our Leader and the knowledge that we are building a better world for all."

BOCA GRANDE 9/1

The law offices of Raymond & Borden occupied three floors in a characterless structure that had gone up on Park Avenue in the decade following World War II. At that time what was important was to build quickly, high enough so that a breathtaking yield in leases might be realized, but not so high that true expertise would be required in the construction.

Henry Raymond, the senior of the senior partners, and Lewis Raymond Flickinger's uncle had agreed to the move from Pine Street. He appreciated irascibly the gain that he and Borden would reap from the sale of their four-story townhouse down there even though he had said, "I'm a lawyer, not a damned real estate speculator!"

And he brought the office suite that his father had used on Pine Street to the new offices.

His interview with the decorator had been very brief.

He had leaned back in his black oak chair with the carved lions on the arms and said, "I'll be in Speonk for three months. When I come back, have it ready. And for every nail hole you put in the paneling I'll put one in you. Remember that.

"One more thing. My kidneys are bad and I want you to put in a toilet somewhere close."

Over the years, Ray Flickinger had made other changes in the firm, but slowly, as the old man withdrew more and more finally from contact with the firm.

It still supervised a number of trusts that belonged to some of the old families, but Ray had recruited more and more corporate specialists and had developed a thriving subsidiary practice in negligence conducted by three young men whose dress and demeanor were outlandish even in times like these.

The firm had become a kind of legal supermarket where one might find counsel for any problem—bankruptcy, proxy fight, eviction, or back injury.

Lovell's place in this shapeless pyramid was never precisely defined, either by himself or anyone else. He had never leaped upward. His progress was rather a slow and steady traverse aided by Ray himself: three years' clerking, four years' corporate litigation, four years' trust management, five years' general stewardship and assistance to Ray working on personnel, management, the new billing system.

He paused rarely to survey his position. When he married; when their son was born; when he became forty.

It was a commitment that seemed to strengthen itself over the years without any real nourishment from either Lovell or Ray Flickinger.

There were tacit understandings, or seemed to be. Nothing was ever spelled out in detail. Advances in income or position arrived before there was any expression from him of need for either money or satisfaction.

Lovell had no more responsibility for the firm's survival than an actor has for his lines.

He worked for it, sometimes at night, occasionally over a weekend. He traveled for it, dined for it, made a social friend for it. But he did not like it. In rare moments of self-consideration he did not approve of it, or of himself.

"If I'm growing," he told Ray one evening on the way to the train, "it's sidewise." He gestured at his stomach. His vest was too tight.

"Buy a pocket watch," Ray told him, "and a chain with seals."

"What you want to do, John," Flickinger said, "is use the society as an instrument, shape it to your own purpose. If it yields enough money and power and position where you are, then you're in the right place. If it doesn't, change it. Change yourself."

He looked down into the bottom of his glass.

"That firm of ours hadn't altered its character or appearance since 1861—almost a century. I could have had the same kind of existence there that old Henry had. Caring for the remaining clients. Marching down to the bank with them to open the safety deposit boxes. Bringing in an honest and upright young man or two—not too bright or able—to help me. Conserving the past endlessly and the money painfully. Depending on old Henry not for counsel and advice, but only on his inclination to hand on his pile and his properties.

"I would have been a kind of janitor, keeping the place swept.

"Here, the way it's turned out we sometimes look like a terrible lot of insurance men"—he grinned—"like a mob of advocates standing outside the Inns of Court and waiting for the day's miscreants to show. But we produce money for ourselves, and more, we're back into the current again. We are part of the times. There's satisfaction in that for me. I can understand why there wouldn't be for you. You've just gone along. You're a second banana."

"Some distinction," Lovell said, dryly.

Flickinger grinned.

"I trust you," he told him soapily. "Everyone needs a man like you. Personally, I think that something's been left out of you. That's what makes you a more decent person. I think that if something happened to me before young Henry is ready to come in you'd see him through and see that he got his chance to keep the place going."

"Would you do the same for me?"

"Of course. There'd be differences in the treatment I'd accord your boy, subtle differences, but they'd be there. I'm being honest."

"What a great luxury that is."

"We've been friends long enough so that you can afford some too."

"Right," said Lovell. He finished his drink and paid their check.

Later, sitting on the train with his newspaper held up before him, he dwelled on the conversation. He looked through it, peering at the hazy future.

But he could not concentrate upon the one time sequence. Scenes from his own past, and even dimmer ones that belonged to his father, appeared and with more clarity than they should have had.

There was his son, on a bright day, standing on the foredeck of *Avatar*, peering with keener eyesight and better knowledge at the lifting breeze and indicating to him that he should put the tiller down to meet it.

"Subtle differences in the treatment I would accord."

"In a pig's asshole," he told himself.

There was his father, sitting at the dinner table. There sat his sister and his mother opposite, near the kitchen door.

There were the glass-doored bookcases between living room and dining room.

There was the meatloaf, small even for four, and the bowl of carrots, mashed carrots sprinkled with parsley. Four baked potatoes. An eight-inch lemon meringue pie on the sideboard.

His mother served. His father could not slice even a meatloaf without swearing.

Lovell passed the plates. His father's fine long fingers tapped the table in a rhythmless accenting of his mood, black and despairing.

"Did you have a good day?" his mother asked, smiling.

"Collections were down again all week," he said. That meant the atmosphere in his office was even more strained—that the few who were left there, lawyers, accountants, clerks, would apply themselves even more determinedly to wheedle, cajole, and threaten those who had bought and not paid; that they would telephone endlessly or climb into their shabby sedans and knock on those gray doors and bring back the crumpled dollars that would keep Associated Collections together for a little longer.

Or there would be one less man at a desk. Perhaps two. Perhaps himself.

"On that point, I agree," Lovell told himself. "Something was left out of me."

He stared out of the window as they left the metropolitan area, past that circle of trash strewn with less abandon as they moved farther: doll and baby carriages, supermarket carts gleaming and rustless, slick tires with fifty-thousand-mile histories, dead rats and dead cats. It was a littoral that delineated the crevasses that separated a society.

His father's uneaten helping made two meatloaf sandwiches for him the next day. It was a good lunch. For a good boy.

He could recall that family's distribution of its income with almost utter exactness. He had known what his father's brown envelope contained to the penny. Not because they had wanted him to know, but simply because the subject was of such vital interest.

He could see them at the table in the kitchen, the envelope in the middle of the white-enameled porcelain top; the four hands, calculating, setting it apart leaf by leaf, so much for the mortgage, again for food, subdivided immediately in his mother's mind to cover the next seven days; and then coal, light, gas, and, lastly, the telephone. He listened.

When his father did look up he set his fingers on two quarters and passed them across the table.

"Your allowance," he said gruffly. "Don't spend it all in one place."

After school the next day his mother would give him the pay envelope, the money to pay the utilities and the bills in it, and he would go and pay them, remembering to wait for the receipts.

He shook himself out of that and into the present. He thought of his present income and how it vanished across the mahogany desk in the study, never seen in dollars, traceable only by the things it left behind in the flow—cars and tires and clothes and lawn furniture. Liquor bottles, tennis lessons, airline tickets, dresses and coats and handsome sweaters, unconsidered gifts, chaises longues, summer camp fees, eighty-five gallons of gasoline a month.

He rarely demurred. The house swelled with possessions. In every corner, in every room, attic, corner cabinet, closet, on shelving and in separate storage bin lay gratifications for the four of them.

That was a measure for a man, this overprovision of paltry goods and insubstantial services.

Nevertheless, a point of abrasion was the portion spent on *Avatar*.

Joyce's finger on the ledger four or five times a year was the indication. If he curtailed that spendthrift obsession, the only one to which he was prey, those two thousands would make a real difference.

"Why is it necessary to have it listed in *Lloyd's Register* every year? It's a silly extravagance."

He rarely responded to the gambit.

He was surprised that so few of his friends had any understanding of why he owned this boat.

He felt that it would have been well beyond his capacity to explain it as something more than an obsession, that its ownership had many positive—even vaulting—advantages, that the benefits were unimaginable: they expanded the horizons for a man; a sense of freedom; extraordinary beauties at almost any time of day or season; a comparative sense of one's physical abilities and impairments as the years passed.

But such explanations were not acceptable from him. He had to live within the presence that he had shown for twenty years and more.

He lived with most of what he was that marks a man—the goodness, the sensitivity to others, the humanity, and the unworthy aberrances all lockered away like a ship's equipment. It occurred to him that he should take an inventory, but suddenly he became very tired and slept the rest of the way home.

On Wednesday, during the last week in August, Lovell met Perkinson at Singapore House, which stands four-square at the foot of a crooked alley that overlooks the Battery and the Verrazano Bridge.

Five stories high and built of brownstone block with beveled edges, it resembles the residence of a Nantucket fleet owner. But this roof is sheathed with copper and there is no widow's walk.

In other times its membership had consisted of shipowners

and perhaps a well-to-do chandler or two. But that has changed over the years, and now the quaintness of its rooms and memorabilia and the excellence of its seafood and fish have attracted a somewhat different membership. Now they are bankers and brokers, oil company executives, real estate counselors, and their confreres. The hours are still struck in ship's bells, and the board that maintains and operates the place is headed by a Commodore who is assisted by various Flag Officers.

Perkinson was waiting for him at a table in the broad and sunny second-floor dining room. He sat beneath a dark oil painting of a barkentine, away in a breeze with foam at her forefoot.

"Very appropriate," Lovell told him.

"Have a sherry," Perkinson said. "I like it better than the hard stuff. If I have two or three martinis, I'm not worth a damn all afternoon."

"Same," Lovell said. "Where are the others?"

"Out of town," Perkinson said. "At each other's throats somewhere." He drew his lips together in a line and shook his head.

"I'll be glad when this is over. You know, in your time it was considerably easier. You didn't have this drift between operations, there was a single focus to the organization.

"Now there's a different atmosphere, last-minute plan changes, analyses. I used to think I had a gift for that."

He shrugged.

"Well. You don't want to hear about that."

"No," Lovell said in agreement. "But maybe I ought to. You know," he said thoughtfully, "your concept is the best part of the affair. It's the best cover imaginable. But that's about the only thing that's good."

Perkinson smiled tolerantly, indicating how long Lovell had been away, how shallow was his understanding.

"Hear me out, Perk. You could have difficulties on the way in and on the return that no one could plan for. A group of disparate individuals—"

"Less disparate than most we see now," Perkinson said. "Compared to some, this is a phalanx."

"Still, you can't use people the way you did in 1944."

He passed his hand vaguely across the top of his glass.

"Politically, philosophically. It's a different time."

"For you too."

"It's not insuperable for me. And I am fully informed."

"The ones who don't respond to Madden's attitude will find their satisfactions in other ways.

"John, this is a small thing. You have been living such a small life for so long—a selfish life really, and I don't mean that in the usual sense—that you don't know how insignificant it is. Nothing big is at stake. Believe me.

"And I'd rather you didn't try to tell me my job. I know what I have to do. You are in or you are out. You have a lot to gain from it. I've done some analysis on you lately, and I know. Besides, the whole thing may turn out to be nothing but a cruise in the sun. And you won't be laying waste to a nation.

"I have a timetable drawn up for you. Do you have a crew? In addition to us?"

"I'm pretty sure."

"What have you told them? Anything?"

"Not yet."

"Don't. Tell them as late as possible. Any fanatics?"

"Not the way you mean."

Perkinson nodded.

"Fine. There's a shipyard on the Chesapeake. They'll pick up your boat toward the end of September and take it down there and start working on it. They want a hull plan. Have you got one? . . . Good. And a sail plan. They need two months before it will be ready for trial. Should be faster, stronger, and so on, and they will furnish all necessary gear. The best."

"I want to see it done," Lovell told him.

"Surely. Whenever you like."

He leaned back in his chair and regarded Lovell thoughtfully.

"John," he said, "just think of it as a windfall. A happy circumstance that suits your needs at the moment. Don't dwell on it. Just take advantage of it and forget it. All right?"

"They need more than two months," Lovell told him. "That's your first mistake. Closer to three. And it won't be right the first time either."

Perkinson waved his hand.

"Not these people. They work out the design changes on a computer and it's on a twenty-four-hour schedule. We operate on the old J. P. Morgan principle—'If you have to ask how much it costs, you can't afford it.'"

He smiled.

"Come on," he said, "behave like a yachtsman. A dozen oysters, and we ought to get a bottle to christen the idea with. What say?"

"Order it," Lovell said simply.

Having eaten so well at lunch, Lovell had little interest in dinner and Joyce's annoyance was apparent.

There were principles that she lived by, and dinner as a family, uninterrupted by telephone calls or other interference, was one.

So between the frenetic weekend activity that began on Friday and wound to a splenetic halt Sunday evening, the four demonstrated their commitment to family life.

It was their strength. Its importance could not be overemphasized.

"How was everyone's day?" Joyce said. It was as familiar a sentence as the opening of Sunday service.

Lovell picked at his chicken salad. Every chunk was absolutely gristle-free. Joyce had prepared it as though doing penance.

He did not hear Nancy's reply. He heard her speak in that cadence that blurred almost all the sense of what she said and found himself hoping for the day when she would offer some detail of exactly how she had spent a long summer afternoon: lying below the gunwales of a Blue Jay, adrift off the end of the inlet, with the top of her blue-flowered bathing suit unfastened, and a trembling and passionate pair of hands all over her.

Jack's turn. He had become more deliberate this past year and his sophistication emphasized the difference in age between his sister and himself. Eighteen months.

Lovell listened, fork poised, and paid flattering attention, trying to draw from this person some hint of what he would become.

There was little that he could discern. There was a smug rejection of much that his father was, and what Jack imagined that he believed, but there was still generosity in his assessment and little of the harshness and blunt antagonism that some of his friends faced.

There were dead spaces between them, certainly, but each could happily remember that they had been father and son in subtle appreciation.

There would be a gulf one day, but not now.

Lovell gnawed at his third ear of corn. Early in their marriage he had told Joyce of his passion for it as a child, when Sunday dinner after a ride in the country was a great bowl of it steaming in the center of the table, husked with care by Lovell, boiled for five minutes in heavily salted water, and eaten immediately with butter churned by that farmer's wife.

Joyce had remembered. She served it from the first of June to the first of September, fresh golden bantam corn that tasted of cold storage at best. The children detested it.

As the summer wore on he was faced with more and more as the price fell. It dripped margarine in concern for Lovell's cholesterol level, but he bore up manfully. Corn-serving was a figure in their minuet.

Beneath the table, Jack glanced at his watch twice and, smiling, waited for his mother to finish her coffee. As the cup hit the saucer he was up and gone with a mumbled good-bye and they were alone.

"Midnight for you, Jack, remember," Joyce told him. And to Nancy, firmly: "Ten-thirty, Nan. No arguments."

Lovell considered the evening.

His after-dinner hours had never been without a pattern and now they were a deep straight channel.

His life did not resemble those tidal flats that he walked on in the winter, full of random curves and underminings, some of surprising depth.

He could drive to the Sound and go aboard *Avatar,* smoke a pipe in the quiet and watch the moon rise. But that would be at the price of the exchange with Joyce.

He might spread his night's supply of papers from his briefcase across the desk in the study and browse away the evening. But Joyce would be using that telephone dispensing advice, or asking it, on slipcover fabrics or a maid, and whether this year they would cruise to Cuttyhunk or Padanaram, or stay at Block Island for the week.

The telephone rang and she went to answer it.

"I'll be back in an hour or so," he told her. "Unless you want to come along."

Her lips twisted in impatience, aware that he had spoken exactly at the sound of the bell.

"No thanks," she told him. "Have a night out."

The night was a brilliant one. An end-of-summer night in its coolness and in the shift of the constellations. The launchman dozed in the cabin above the little bridge that led to the club marina and the docking floats.

Lovell did not wake him. He was an old man of quick temper and given to sudden and unaccountable rages. In payment for his years of service—he was too old to qualify for the pension plan the members had been finally forced to adopt for their retainers—he had been given this sinecure, for which he was not grateful. At eighty-two he spoke his mind too often.

He was a point of issue between two groups. One, to which Ray Flickinger belonged, wanted to be rid of him forever. But the other, a group of ancients who remembered when the crews of racing sailboats were made up of paid Norwegians, was implacable.

Ray had made no secret of his opposition to Captain Foley.

There had been a Sunday afternoon when the four of them had returned from a weekend cruise. Ray was badly sunburned, had wrenched his ankle picking up the mooring, and parched for drink.

Constance Flickinger and Joyce were thus overladen with the unused supplies and clothing and staggered under their burdens.

Ray limped ahead, and when he glanced back at them, Captain Foley was standing, untipped for weeks, at the wheel of the launch and icily inattentive.

"Goddamn it!" Ray said suddenly, "drop that crap there! Let Foley carry it up!"

The three of them paused then and Ray gestured again, peremptorily, as though calling a rickshaw boy. Lovell saw the red suffuse Foley's neck beneath his tan and flood his face to the roots of his hair.

"Foley doesn't carry crap!" he shouted. "Foley's no goddamn bellboy, and don't you forget it!"

Ray turned back to him, his eyes popping from his head. He threw the armful of heavy weather gear on the float.

"You son of a bitch," he said clearly. "I've had all I'll ever take from you." He limped back toward the launch but Constance was in front of him, pushing her burden at his chest.

"Stop," she said crisply. "Stop it right now. You're not to say any more."

Ray turned again and limped away. In the bar his hand trembled as he raised his glass and finally he excused himself and went away to phone one of the club officers.

Surprisingly, Foley treated Lovell with some deference, either to maintain a foot in some part of the enemy's camp or as an example of his own magnanimity. Nonetheless, Lovell asked little from him, and then only after long preparation.

Lovell walked down the gangway and sat in the stern of the club launch.

The harbor waters were almost still. Infrequently a runabout moved past, her wake faintly phosphorescent. The moon appeared in the southern sky, an enormous bitter orange circle. There were well-defined elevations across its whole surface.

Thirty feet away, in the marina area, there was a sudden splashing and a squeak of panic.

Above, the cabin door opened and Foley stood silhouetted in the door. He flashed a powerful hand lantern below him where the gold platers spent the summer, rocking gently in their finger slips.

There was a rat struggling in the dark water, threshing, squeaking, and below it, a boil and bulge from some pursuer.

"Look at that son of a bitch," said Foley in awe. "Striper. I seen him every night this week. God, what a fish."

The rat made at whatever speed it could for the end of the nearest slip, but that was an agonizing distance and the tide was against it.

This time Lovell saw the shape of the fish just below the surface. It struck with a shock that was almost palpable to him.

Both shapes were gone. Away at a distance a silvery school of baitfish flickered in the harbor lights and disappeared. In the remaining ripples the moored yachts bowed and fell still.

"You see that?" the old man said hoarsely, his voice rising.

Lovell leaned over the side to peer at the dark water.

He would not go out to his boat tonight. There would be no satisfaction in it. It was not his any more, not the same ship that promised him a voyage of realization.

Now it was an instrument, a vehicle with an aim and a use to which he had committed it, himself, and his friends.

For the first time, he wondered how they would benefit.

"Unending vigilance is the price we must pay for our
liberty. We may not rest, not the humblest either,
for all of us and Our Leader himself must watch and
prepare for the unknown ahead."

BOCA GRANDE 9/25

The twentieth of September that year, Lovell entered the annual "Whalers' Race." Frank Colleran and Max Berliner were aboard and their occasional spinnaker man and foredeck operative, Charlie Iacovino.

The day was delightful and the race was different enough and casual enough so that there was reason to enter *Avatar*.

Merely having Iacovino aboard gave them more confidence, for Charlie was much in demand on better boats. Sure-footed, enormously strong, and experienced, he was worth an hour to the rating.

It was he who chose their anchorage and set the small Danforth.

With enough scope, it held *Avatar* and they furled

the sails and made halliards and rigging ready for the starting gun.

Having arrived at the line early and taken such a good position, there was time to relax and enjoy the day. They calculated the breeze, listened to the weather on the VHF, and watched as more and more entrants appeared.

At first gun there were almost a hundred, from twenty-foot one-designs to their nearest neighbor to port, a beamy old cutter fifty feet at the waterline with a main gaff the size of a yule log. A swarm of children were aboard her from bowsprit to bumpkin.

They lowered a Navy anchor and paid out chain as though expecting Force 10.

The day sparkled brightly, the water a clear and gleaming blue. These were the days they waited for, with mixed emotions, these September and October days when the weather changed with exquisite subtlety, the seas retaining the warmth of summer and the breeze turning more to the west and north quadrants and building to regular ten- and twenty-knot strengths.

Iacovino saw to everything twice and still could not bring himself to sit down with them in the cockpit. He went to the bow again and examined the anchor line and checked the sheets and halliards once more. Then he sprayed the spinnaker pole fittings with his little pressure can of silicon.

Lovell turned the tiller over to Colleran for the start and Iacovino leaned down from midships to discuss the starting tactic.

"We'll come off on starboard tack just as soon as John has the genoa up," he said. "You just start sailing and keep bearing off as you go until we get a head of steam up."

"Charlie," Max said, "just one yell from you if the halliard is foul or something. Just one. Not a lot of screaming so I don't set the sheets to no purpose."

"No purpose!" Iacovino sneered. "Christ, what language."

The ten-minute gun was fired. On board the committee boat a white cylinder went up.

Next to them on the cutter a group set to work at shortening the rode. They hauled in a fathom of one-inch manila and it fell in coils about their ankles. No one seemed to notice as they strained away.

"Get your goddamn feet out of those coils!" Iacovino bawled at them suddenly. They paused and gaped at him.

"Never mind him," their helmsman shouted to his foredeck, "he's trying to upset you."

"Well I'm a son of a bitch," said Iacovino, unbelieving. He started back toward *Avatar*'s stern, puffing with righteous rage.

"Forget it, Charlie," Lovell told him.

"Those kids will lose their legs in that goddamn line!"

Lovell shaded his eyes and looked at the masthead fly. There was no wind shift in the offing, it seemed.

"Just be glad they aren't yours."

It was so typical of Iacovino to behave in this manner, Lovell thought.

Iacovino the *pater familias*. Father of nine children, all of them brought up in the Roman Catholic consuetude that seems to be the only American contribution to the faith.

All observed every ritual, all made every obeisance in charge of Iacovino's wife, who dressed normally in black and went to mass every morning of her life. Iacovino paid every service that his ready lip could manage to this method of child-rearing.

He spent no weekends at home from May until the end of October. He was gone again on an endless series of races from February until April.

In the decade that he had spent racing sailboats and mastering his esoteric specialty he had come to watch over the children of others with an overwhelming solicitude that fortified his own self-regard. Thus satisfied, he continued on his way, getting another of his own yearly, like a Genoese waiter serving on a cruise ship.

Of his nine children, eight had birthdays in October.

Discussing that month of birthdays, Colleran had counted carefully back on his fingers and tried to arrive at a conclusive reason.

"I think," he said, "that he only gets laid once a year—New Year's Day."

The five-minute gun sounded. Colleran worked the tiller lightly. Lovell took his position at the main halliard winch and ground up the slack in the wire. In the cockpit Max cleared the genoa sheets beside both winches and stood watching Iacovino.

Charlie crouched like a boxer, opening and closing his hands.

"Three minutes," Colleran called out, and from the others along the ragged line, bow to bow, other times were called.

"Two minutes."

Iacovino knelt on the foredeck and lifted the anchor line out of the bow chock. Colleran stood up and raised the tiller to hip level. Max took two turns around the drum of the genoa winch.

"One minute," Colleran said, and then he called the seconds, first by tens and then by fives. At thirty seconds Lovell ground up the mainsail, glanced up once at the headboard, seated where it should be on its mark, braked the winch, stepped across the front of the mast, and reached for the winch handle to hoist the genoa jib.

It wasn't there.

It was minutes it seemed before he could find it lying in the scuppers near the rail.

Iacovino was hauling great bights of the anchor line in,

with first a grunt as though struck in the stomach by a bat and then a succession of profane bellows.

"The genoa," he shouted, "get it up, goddamn it! Will you get it up, for Christ's love! Get it up, you dumb bastard!"

And Max in his anxiety hauled in the genoa sheet so tightly that the foot of the sail was stretched like the skin of a drum, and Lovell, even after he had retrieved the winch handle, could not hoist the sail beyond halfway, heave though he might.

"Sail on the main, set the main then goddamn it," Iacovino shrieked. "Fall off, fall off, and fill it. Slack the sheet!" he screamed at Max.

Max did, at once, and the sail went up to the block and flapped and filled as Colleran held her off. They had way on and inched their way up to the orange flag that marked the end of the starting line.

There was a boat across already, farther up the line, and another and yet another. Then they were there, but they had calculated the distance too closely and had not accounted for their minor delay.

As Frank bore off to clear the flag there was a small thud at the quarter and another near the stern.

"You hit the son of a bitch," Iacovino hissed, "didn't you?"

"I didn't," Frank told him, "we did."

Astern, the flag bobbed up from the contact. There was no one to see it save the cutter and her child crew.

"Forget it," said Iacovino, "get her going. We'll quit later when we see how we do. Come on, get some life into her."

The other three looked at each other, temporizing. The question of how to handle it might be decided in several ways. Hitting a mark in this race was penalized heavily.

There was sudden treble calling from the cutter, still worrying away at her Navy anchor, her main gaff jammed halfway up the mast and a storm jib hooked awry to her forestay.

"They hit the mark," came the chorus, and at once a red protest flag three feet square appeared in her starboard rigging. It was the only well-handled hoist on the whole boat. The helmsman was pointing a finger at them as they bore away, an accusing finger. For emphasis, he bent his arm and snapped it out again and again as they sailed away.

Two hours after the start, Lovell took the tiller and Frank Colleran stretched and went forward on the windward side to relieve Iacovino in calling the set of the genoa to the helm.

Lovell settled himself to leeward, leaning forward, his body parallel to the lubber line of *Avatar,* right hand behind him, balancing the gracefully curved tiller, steering with the seas, seeking that accommodation among sails, sea, breeze, and hull that would mean that he was moving the boat at her best speed.

There were ten miles before them before they turned the next mark and Iacovino could set the spinnaker. He came back to the cockpit, muttering.

He peered blackly across *Avatar's* beam at a group of boats upwind and inshore of them.

"They're wiping you," he said bitterly. "You should have tacked. At least you'd be in the same breeze."

Lovell grunted. Iacovino's pronouns varied exactly with occurrence. If the breeze were to head the inshore boats, it would be "we" who were wiping them. Sailing with him was a two-edged sword with the keener edge facing his captain.

"I'm going to Jamaica this year," Lovell said suddenly. "What about you people?"

"In what?" Colleran asked.

Lovell tapped the coaming next to him.

"This."

Max grinned.

"Who died?"

"She's going to be redesigned and refitted, completely," Lovell said, squinting at the telltales on the weather shrouds.

Iacovino leaned forward, lifted one thigh from the cushion, and farted.

"You'd have to dig up Nat Herreshoff to do that job. Right, Maxie baby?"

He pinched Max's calf.

"That's not your problem," Lovell told him brusquely. He wondered how many important decisions must be made in this way. A blurted phrase, habit, and proximity were of more weight than a thought process.

"I'm going," Max said immediately. "Who else have you got?"

"I just signed the articles," Colleran told him. "When do I report? It must be a reward for service. Like a leave."

"Who's going besides us?" Max asked. "We have to have at least six, don't we?"

"Got them. One is a navigator, but you bring your sextant anyhow, Max."

"What about you, Charlie? Yes or no?"

"You fucking captains are all alike," Iacovino said idly. "Get a few bucks together and you're pushing."

Lovell smiled, abashed, and Iacovino indicated his experience.

"You pay all expenses?"

"Christ sake," Max said in disgust.

Iacovino went on inexorably.

"Plane ticket?"

Lovell nodded.

"Everything's on me."

"Bar bills?"

"Everything."

"You have to get things settled before you go. Went from

Buenos Aires to Rio with a cheap prick once. We broke our humps and he wound up with a third in class. Know what we got for it? A ball-point pen with the name of the boat on it. And that's all.

"You know him, Max? Freedman was his name. I think he was a landsman of yours."

Max eyed him coldly.

"Yeah, I know him," he said. "We're all related. Abraham was our father."

"What are you so sensitive about? I thought you'd think it was funny. You have to know what kind of shipmates you've got. What you can say and what you can't say. Isn't that so, John?"

He did not wait for Lovell to agree.

"Sure you do. Like, how do I know you aren't bringing a Greek along who'll sneak into my bunk some dark night and have his way with me?"

Having recruited them, Lovell listened to them with half an ear. The crew was set, he had accomplished so much. Iacovino was certainly a mate for Madden. Colleran dovetailed with Perkinson. Max and Amat had more in common than either would admit readily.

That left only the captain.

The captain who had the command, but neither the will to nor the ability to pretend that he had. The person who had schooled himself with painstaking care in the lore and knowledge of seafarers from the time of the Old Testament.

From Simon the Fisherman to Joshua Slocum and on to the cruising captains and the record-keepers who fought the seas and their own boredom in smaller and smaller boats on longer and longer voyages.

One day one of them would circumnavigate in a kayak on vitamin pills and a portable conversion still.

All of them with a purpose that was finer than his. There

was nothing in his adventure that was higher than base or broader than unmoral.

The politics were unimportant; at worst, little better than organized vandalism.

"You're wandering, Captain," Colleran said. "Head up a little."

It was a game like all others played around him in every facet of his society and his time. A game that he dabbled in with nine tenths of himself—or whatever proportion was necessary to ensure the benefit that was sought.

Ah, but this was a different game from most. This one offered enough money and enough power and enough testing of strength and endurance.

And there were other advantages: freedom of movement, sensual pleasures heretofore beyond his grasp. Those were there.

He was a lesser being, Lovell. But having spared himself so little, he thus strengthened his resolve and his commitment. Having admitted his own commonness as a man, he could do nothing else than certify it. Any other attitude confirmed him in hypocrisy.

When they rounded the windward mark, after struggling endlessly against a foul tide and a fading breeze, they set their spinnaker.

Iacovino curled his lip in disgust.

"Don't forget to save some money for sails," he said. "This thing's got more rip stop in it than nylon."

The first of the fleet was already hull down on the horizon, losing itself in the haze along the shore. Astern, there was a smaller group, light-displacement hulls ghosting along under whisker-poled jibs, closing the distance between themselves and *Avatar* slowly, inexorably. Farther astern still, but close enough to see clearly was the bottom of the fleet, the cutter that was protesting them prominent there, her red flag hanging limp from the starboard stay.

"Pick a course, for Christ's sake," Iacovino said in disgust.

He stood just before the mast, moving the spinnaker pole gently with one hand, holding the limp sheet in the other and staring at each luff in turn for any encouraging flutter.

"Can't even jibe the fucker," he mumbled.

Max and Colleran looked for breeze, for any cat's-paw, but there was none, only an oily sea and a faint swell from the east that brought nothing with it.

They dragged along, rolling, the main sheet rigging slapping in the swell at the middle section of the strung-out boom.

"Down south there'll be breeze," Max said.

Colleran agreed, a parade of images from the yachting magazines in his head.

"Fifteen to twenty all day long."

"Come on," Iacovino said, "let's quit this goddamn drifting match and go home. This is no race. Besides, we're going to get thrown out anyhow."

Lovell looked at the others, questioning them silently.

They shrugged; their new stature had already made a difference.

"Okay," Lovell said. "But it's the last race we ever leave. Anybody who doesn't feel that way, say so now."

Ashore, Lovell telephoned the race committee chairman and gave his name and told him that *Avatar* had withdrawn.

"We hit the starting mark," he said.

The chairman grunted.

"I wish there were more like you," he said.

"Forward we march in victorious mettle, from one glorious exploit to another. We put behind us our military triumph. Now we shall win that economic victory that they have told us for centuries we could not do!"
BOCA GRANDE 10 / 6

The tidewater area of Virginia, some fifty-odd miles outside of Washington, is a serene and lovely area. In early October the low hills that line the shores of the Potomac Delta are still lush and green, the countryside is still scented with the long summer, and only on the weekends when the city dwellers strike for the coasts are there many people in evidence.

*Avatar* was in a large and almost deserted shipyard some thirty miles from Fredericksburg.

The sign over the gate was recently painted: "Jensen & Lofgren, Shipwrights." The vane on the top of the main office shone in the late sunshine. There were numbers of hulls snugged down in their cradles and covered for the winter already, but Lovell, thinking of the bow-to-stern storage in his own usual winter situation where one could barely find room to sand the stem, was surprised that so well equipped and maintained a yard was not full.

He found Jensen in a large and airy office behind a mahogany desk that seemed to have been built out of ship's planking. The desk, and indeed all the other furniture, had been painstakingly sanded and varnished to a finish like glass.

He admired it and Jensen responded with a smile.

"You could sail this desk better than most boats, uh?" he said. "Most they make today, anyhow, uh?"

Lovell asked if he could see *Avatar*.

"Sure," Jensen told him. "A patient, uh. We haven't done nothing to her yet but take everything off, uh. You made lots of make-do repairs yourself, uh?"

Lovell admitted that he had.

"We could tell. You spend fifteen years with me, I could make you a carpenter, maybe, uh? Some of them are not bad. Even where they don't show. That's the mark of a good worker, uh? Not a plumber."

"How long will it take you to do what's going to be done?" Lovell asked him.

"No schedule yet. Today the engineer and his helper are down there. Two days they were here this week, uh? Engineers. That's for building ore boats, engineers. Or a tanker. So many tons go in here, so many come out here. So much weight on the cargo boom here, so much power in the winches, uh? For this job you need a shipbuilder, not an engineer, uh?"

Lovell nodded and asked for directions.

"Go to the rigger's shed," Jensen said, "and then to the left. She's by herself in the shed beyond. I'll come down later after I talk to the insurance." He stood up.

"Insurance. He hit the fuel dock in Lewisetta Saturday. Stove the bow in. His broker tells me to patch it. I told him, 'You don't patch that. You scarf those planks and refasten for ten feet aft and you feather the paint after you do the planking. Six coats of paint. Takes the carpenter twenty hours, the painter ten hours, uh? If you want it patched, take it to a tailor, uh?' "

*Avatar* was in a new cradle and stripped of all fittings, her hull washed clean from rail to keel. There were four ladders and a scaffold system all around, and two men had her sail and hull plans spread upon a tall drafting table in a corner.

Lovell introduced himself.

The engineer was a wispy fellow named Grant. He didn't bother to introduce his assistant.

"What do you think?" said Lovell a trifle expansively, still pleased by Jensen's compliment about his abilities.

"About what?" said Grant.

"The boat. *Avatar*."

"What I think is you've got problems," said Grant. The assistant nodded dolefully.

"Problems," he repeated.

"But not insoluble," Grant said.

"Not really insoluble," said the assistant.

"What's the most you've ever gotten out of her?" Grant asked him.

Lovell mused. He remembered the needle on the Kenyon flickering at eight knots. He said so.

"You were probably on a broad reach with the spinnaker set and a breeze of over twenty. Right?"

"I guess so."

"Well, when we finish you'll have a faster boat. There's only so much we can do, but the computer is a big help. We'll reduce the quarter wave, change the bow so it will lift instead of plow, and increase the fore triangle."

"Hopefully," said the assistant.

"But there's only so much you can do." He shook his head and frowned at *Avatar*.

"Trouble with the people who built those things is that they depended on their intuition. Esthetics, not mathematics. Boat design is simply a mathematical equation. That's not our way. We'll change all that."

"When will you begin?" Lovell said, dryly.

"Oh, we'll have all the information in a couple of days," Grant said. "Then it's just a matter of taking the output and applying it to your plan and turning that over to Jensen and letting him translate. No problem."

"But how will it sail?" Lovell asked. "Differently?"

"Very," Grant told him. "Very differently. You better allow a little time for trials."

"Expensive?" Lovell asked.

"Very. But that doesn't concern me."

"This isn't your usual job?"

Grant shook his head firmly.

"Certainly isn't. High-speed amphibious hulls are my field. You borrowed me. But it's all the same to me. Merely application of the same information to a different purpose."

"Who will supervise the construction?" Lovell asked him quietly.

"You can leave all that to Jensen. It will save a lot of argument. He'll have complete drawings, and he'll execute them exactly. That's why we're here. He talks like an ark builder, but he does what we tell him to do. Grumbles and complains, but he translates properly. We had that out with him years ago."

Grant smiled to himself.

"The year before he started working with us, he had a thirty-thousand-dollar loss. Now he has a nice little business and he's got time to varnish his office furniture."

He put out his hand.

"Good luck," he said, and they departed, the assistant having folded up the plans and tucked everything away in a brief-case.

"Good luck," he echoed, and they were gone.

Rays of the setting sun shone down through the windows in the upper wall of the shed, motes of wood dust danced in the breeze from the doorway.

Lovell climbed to *Avatar's* deck level. She looked longer in here, almost massive, but characterless and empty beyond the absence of spar and boom, running rigging, winches, and the alterations he had made for his own convenience.

The bolt holes under the port winch were still damp and soft. The deck canvas had blistered. The binocular case that he had made four winters ago was gone.

He remembered Jack helping to paint the bilges, reaching head down to the limit of his ten-year-old's arms with a rag on the end of a stick, and how he had spent forty minutes cleaning the paint splotches off his forehead with vegetable oil rather than turpentine.

For reward, dinner at the Italian restaurant. A pizza and a great bowl of spaghetti.

"That was a good job well done," he had told him solemnly, and Jack had agreed with a self-effacing blush of pride.

He descended. Jensen was standing outside, smoking a pipe with a curved stem and looking out across the wide river mouth toward the sea.

"You met Mr. Grant, uh? You look like I feel when I talk to Mr. Grant. He knows, Mr. Grant, uh. How to make boats and space stations too. He should stick to space stations, uh?"

Lovell was noncommittal. He wanted no allies beyond his present ones.

Jensen looked at him curiously and pried a little, perhaps seeking companionship.

His yard was a scrim. This Norwegian boatbuilder was a

creature whose living was arranged for him by a clerk in the bottom of a concrete pile eighty miles away.

"Why do you come all the way down here by tow, uh," asked Jensen, "when you have twenty yards nearby, and turn your boat over to a little man like him?"

"He's a friend of a friend," Lovell said simply.

"Your boat won't be the better for it," Jensen told him. "Or you either, uh?"

"I 'won't be the better for it either, uh?'" Lovell told himself, driving back toward Fredericksburg in the soft twilight, and shrugged his shoulders in rejection.

The specific beauty of the evening, together with the evidence of Perkinson's care and planning, the competence, the assumption of detail, engendered a sense of well-being.

It was like a child's world: simple, authoritarian, without harsh discipline. There were even additional pleasures. In this world he was both child and master.

The sun was now low in the foothills to his left as he followed the road to the north. On the shore side there were few houses, perhaps an occasional wink of light or a reflection of the sun's last bright rays on a window. Then he came to a bluff, a wide expanse of acreage, as the road curved away toward a town.

Here, far back from the road, was a graceful house with a center section three stories high and two lesser wings balanced in window, shutter, and roof line.

There was a sign set in the trimmed boxwood at the gate. "Inn" it read simply in black Roman letters.

On impulse he turned into the drive. The reverie into which he had fallen had conjured up not only this place but a series of half-dreams, half-wishes. For Lovell there was no other turn to make on this whole seacoast.

Once in England he had seen a place like it suffering neither the weight of some decorator's matched quaintnesses nor bearing up under the strain of an unseen headquarters that shipped the meals frozen and sealed from a central warehouse and marked all the bar glass to a scribed line.

His room was well furnished. There were logs and kindling lying on the hearth. The small-paned windows gave upon a limitless view over the estuary beyond the wide gardens below.

At seven the dining room was surprisingly crowded for an evening in midweek, yet the room, despite its low, beamed ceiling, was quiet without being subdued.

On the way to his table he passed a mahogany cupboard with an open front fitted up as a wine rack. There were three vintages set forth together with a small card. He stopped a moment to read: "These are the wines we recommend to accompany the entrées on our menu tonight."

He drank two martinis before dinner. Each was crisp and dry and served in a footed glass. He had a bottle of Meursault with his sea bass for dinner and found himself euphoric after half the bottle was gone. He conducted an unspoken dialogue with himself on the strength of it.

"A clean and sparkling room, a good meal, well served from cracker to table-crumbing, enough alcohol and no companionship is all that the silent traveler can ask.

"All that is needed is resource, the psychological completeness to admit the selfishness of the personality.

"No consequence is important. That is for the law and/or the civilization to mull over later.

"Let this powerful presence that is 'I' remain. Let it last beyond this night and far on."

He finished the bottle, unaffected, he knew, except that his speech to the waiter and the white-haired man who stood behind the reception desk was slightly slurred and affected.

"I should like," he told him carefully, "to come back from time to time, and should like to make a reservation for the same room, perhaps every other weekend beginning on the first of the month. I shall cancel by midweek if it should not be possible to come down from New York. How can we conclude this arrangement?"

He moved back half a pace from the counter, standing comfortably, without any reinforcing slump over the desk, without smoking, without his hands in his pockets.

"Oh, that can be easily arranged," the clerk told him. "Would you like the same room?"

"Indeed I would," Lovell told him definitely. Then, combining delicacy, forthrightness, and purpose, he added, "There's one thing; there may be other people with me, perhaps one, perhaps more. So we should keep the arrangement as flexible as possible."

"Of course," said the clerk. "Then you might need a connecting room or a neighboring room also."

"Of course," said Lovell. "That is what I meant. Thank you."

"Thank you, sir," said the clerk with a small smile. "We are happy that you like it here."

Lovell climbed the stairs to his room. In his corridor he paused, his key in the lock, to watch a black maid walking with a lithe stride away from him. Hungrily he listened to the rustle of her skirts.

He lay in his bed, unwilling to let the day end.

Finally he did turn over and eventually he fell asleep.

The following Tuesday at eleven, Ray Flickinger spoke to him on the interoffice telephone.

"Damn it," he said without preliminary, "can you come to lunch with Constance and me? I'm going to have to break away in the middle and we're supposed to talk seriously."

"What's so serious?" he asked.

"Nothing," Ray told him. "She thinks it's serious. One of her ideas."

Ray walked swiftly, gesturing, the tails of his topcoat flapping, adding more details to the Flickinger view of life. To Lovell it was a chore, sometimes onerous, when more was required than merely his presence; when a grunt of agreement was not enough; when a commitment and a corollary statement were needed.

Now Lovell was opposing. He listened to the details, paying more attention, as though preparing notes for the draft of a brief.

It was the congressional race in their district. Constance had decided that she would not support the incumbent. His opponent, whom she had heard by chance, had made a statement that was eminently sensible.

"You're all intelligent people. Ask yourselves if you want your views expressed by someone who is your equal. If not, you don't deserve the franchise."

This summation had so appealed to Constance's idealization of the American Congress as an overgrown town meeting based on New England Protestantism, Middle Western earthiness, and West Coast pioneer spirit that she had thrown her energies into the campaign. Now she wanted money.

"Just a goddamn idiocy," Ray told him. "Congress is pressure groups. They don't sit around deliberating. They buy and sell. Trade and barter, that's their game, and Farrell works it just fine. He was born to it like some people were born to be harness-makers. I've been on his finance committee for the last twelve years. How in the hell does it look?"

He waved his hand in disgust.

She was waiting for them at the restaurant—Ray's present favorite. To Ray, obsequiousness was more important than food. He could tolerate a certain amount of familiarity from his restaurateurs, but since he never gave a proper demarcation, sooner or later the bounds were overstepped and he took himself elsewhere.

Meanwhile, Gino's was in favor and Lovell was hopeful of

an end to it: the icy *moules* that pained the nerves of his teeth, their oily aftertaste, the overdone, overthick slabs of veal that were called *piccata,* the overtipped waiters who hung about brushing and picking threads from his clothing as though ashamed of the overpayment themselves. They offered not service but servility.

There was a Campari and soda before Constance and she was tapping her fingers impatiently. She looked very efficient today in her town suit, but not very agreeable when Lovell appeared, and only softened a bit when he told her that he had come in his official capacity as Family Court Judge.

Ray read the menu and twisted a half turn to the right and another half to the left and muttered a whole sentence before the maître d' came to beg for the privilege of bringing a drink.

Lovell affected that joviality and lightness of tone that was the reason for his presence, but he did not bring it off. He had little opportunity to do so.

"It seems to me," Ray said, opening the discussion, "that you're getting an awful lot of change-of-life ideas these days."

She looked at him with admirable directness and cool self-control.

"What's a 'change-of-life idea'?"

Lovell waited also. Ray glanced at him with annoyance.

"In the first place, politics isn't arguable. Not between us. I make the decisions just as I make the business decisions. You've got enough to do in your area without this. I respect your job and the way you do it."

It had taken a great effort for him to produce this statement, evidenced by the way he had clipped off the words.

"You still haven't made your first point clear," she told him quietly, "and you are a lawyer."

"And this, darling, is not a courtroom."

"Both of you are out of bounds," Lovell said, glancing from

one to the other. "From experience, it's going to turn into a wrangle and I'll have to go to the bar."

A twist of the head or the shake of Constance's wrist, gold bracelets agleam, had brought a waiter. He hovered.

"How are the *moules* today," Lovell asked. "Frozen and well sanded?"

"When I want to order, I'll call you," Ray told him. He retired in confusion. "Goddamn this joint anyway," he said. "You'd think I was investing in it."

"If you were," Constance said, returning to her subject, "I wouldn't argue with you."

"I'm not arguing with you!" he told her. "How the hell does it look if I'm chairman of Farrell's finance committee and you give DiCarlo three thousand dollars? It looks like I've got a foot in both camps."

"You always do," she said. "Sometimes three. It is my money. Isn't it?"

"Be careful. That has not a goddamn thing to do with it. And you know it. When did I ever deny you anything?"

She leaned far back in her chair. Her long fingers spread along the edge of the table. Lovell looked at them and quickly away to a painting of a round-faced gondolier with a mouth like a pink hole.

There he focused his attention while the battle raged across the table.

That battle was the particular expression of the married state. There was evidence that they were both lovers and friends. There were children, observed approaches and aftermaths that Lovell had noticed. But there were also gaps in their relationship, where each lived for a time without reference to or care about the other, pursuing sensations and experiences that were and would remain with each alone.

He was aware of some of Ray's and he was able to surmise

some of Constance's. Until now he was decent enough in his role of friend of both to support the privacy of both. But no longer.

He ordered another round and sipped away. Constance had left hers untouched. Two more Camparis were in a rank next to the first one while the waiter agonized about removing the two and, of course, which two. He consulted the maître d', who paced two paces forward and two back and pretended indifference.

"The trouble with you," Ray said, "is you don't know how to compromise. You've never had to. I've seen to that."

He brooded for a moment, to dwell on the masterly manner he had picked his way through his business life.

"I compromise when it's necessary," she told him. "Not because it's a way of life. It seems to be your whole existence."

At this, Ray withdrew himself utterly from the scene. He became icy and distant and punctilious in comportment. The flush of anger faded from his face and the passion disappeared.

He glanced at his watch.

"I have a meeting at two," he said. "Take the check, John, please. Constance, I expect you know enough not to bring it up again."

"Thank you for your time," she said, and gave him a thin, sour smile.

Happily for the waiter, she solved one immediate difficulty.

"Take these sodas away," she told him, "and bring me a martini."

Her mood changed slowly, the annoyance, the petulance disappeared, and another Constance came to view, warmer, even pliant. An unvoiced communion rose that was based upon previous proximities. The figures in the minuet were now different.

She spoke of it first and, characteristically, with directness.

"You know, old friend," she said, "that something is happening. I don't think I like it. Too much trouble."

He nodded.

"I do."

She picked up her handbag and reached in a sweeping motion for her gloves.

"That's enough for me," she said decisively. "I'm leaving while I still have my decoration. Even though it's not very meaningful any more to anyone but me and 'the Mister.'"

He grinned, pleased that conjecture and his daydream had so coincided.

"Wait a second," he said, savoring this pleasure, this first emergence of a sensual promise. "Let's look at it."

She shook her head definitely.

"That's what the bookstore man said to me one day when I was fourteen and looking up 'cunnilingus' in his dictionary. He came right up behind me and showed me that thing of his. Ugh."

He laughed again, thickly, his collar and tie tight and constricting.

"Awful," she said calmly, leaning a hand beneath her chin. "You even sound like him. My mother told me when you hear that choked laugh, you've gone too far already."

"Very wise woman, your mother. Very fine man, your father. Fine, fine people. You're a credit to their genes. You should have listened. Not that it matters. I'm the one who's gone too far already."

She flicked his glass delicately with her forefinger.

"Just that," she said. "Forget it." She rose swiftly and forestalled him from rising with a hand on his shoulder.

"Thanks for coming. I appreciated it." Then she was gone, threading her way through the tables gracefully.

He sat back in his chair, lower lip between his teeth. The room was almost empty now. He glanced from table to table, looking for another situation like his own. He saw none.

Everywhere else was the promise of success. He drew complex patterns on the cloth with the edge of his glass and considered another drink. There was a heaviness about his thought and a flickering of anger at her and at himself. He saw the two of them with a certain clarity, a post-coital view, merciless, exacerbating.

He bowed his head and shook it in pain, and when he raised it again, she was sitting down again with that same grace, next to him but closer.

She picked up a menu and scanned it quickly.

"It just occurred to me that I hadn't had lunch," she said calmly. "And with all those martinis and your conversation, I was too flushed to walk around town. So I'm back."

"Nice to see you again," he said. "But the match is over. I'm a terrible fencer."

She licked her lips consciously.

"Well then," she said quietly, "I guess we will have to go right to the mat."

"Join us in fraternal kinship we say to our Brothers to the south. We shake your hands warmly and welcome your resistance to the Octopus that has dominated all of us for so long."

BOCA GRANDE 10 / 27

Lovell returned to Virginia again in the last week of October. *Avatar* looked like a hulk. There were major structural changes in both hull and deadwood. The graceful transom that had borne her nameboard was gone, lopped off. The planking at the turn of the bilge was gone too, for the length of the hull. She looked like a carcass, dead on a tide flat.

"This is the worst time of the job, uh," Jensen told him. "From now it gets better." He brought him with a hand on Lovell's elbow to a rack of lumber.

"Look here," he said proudly, "cedar for the new planking. We edge glue it, like a cup boat, uh? Good for years. Feel it," he commanded.

Lovell ran a finger along a plank, tentatively.

"Great," he said, without conviction.

"You bet, great," Jensen said. "When we finish you won't see a seam in that hull, uh? And she will be a thousand pounds lighter.

"The cedar is my idea. The designer, he wants fiberglass—make a mold, pour, cure, all in a month. Then he wants aluminum, uh? I told him, 'If you want aluminum, go to Pittsburgh. I know what I can do. I don't run no goddamn auto factory. I'm no bicycle-maker. Here we make boats, uh? With wood, if she sails sideways we can change it. And we are ready to try her in a month or five weeks.' So he agrees, finally.

"But the spar and boom I can't fight about. Aluminum with interior halliards. It will sound like a pipe foundry but we do our best. Now maybe we get a hull speed three or four knots better. But downwind she will steer like a horse with no reins. Downwind you have to be careful, uh?"

Lovell nodded and nodded again. For all the number of men at work in and around the hull there was little noise. There was a confusion of wood clamps and glue pots. There was an aged and gnarled creature at work on the stem with an adze. He wielded it so expertly that it made no more sound than a cabinetmaker's block plane. The chips eased away across the timber with perfect precision.

Jensen sighed and indicated the old man with the adze.

"Not any more like him around," he said. "When he goes, we use a power saw, uh."

Lovell commiserated.

"He's got a son forty-eight years old. He ran from the old man thirty years ago. Paul. He's a purchasing agent in Richmond now. But there's a grandson here now. Sometimes it skips a generation. He came out of the Navy and asked me to be a rigger, uh. That's the only time I saw the old man smile in thirty years, when the boy went to work here. Every day they eat lunch together and play cribbage, uh. A good boy and a good rigger. He never forgets a cotter pin."

Lovell stayed on for an hour more, alone, and watched. As he did, he knew a certain assurance, a measure of confidence that flowed from the rare skills of Jensen's people. *Avatar* was no hulk, it was a reincarnation.

He had sworn to stay there until three-thirty. Constance was not scheduled to arrive in King William until almost five, but the minutes ticked away so slowly that he could not stay. It would take five minutes just to get out of Jensen's parking lot and back to the road, certainly. There would be Friday traffic, perhaps a load of hay that would delay him. Too, her bus might be early. He savored the sight of her in the doorway, pausing on the step, peering through her sunglasses at him.

As it happened, there was no traffic on the road. There were no mishaps. He was there at four-fifteen and surprised at one point—the speedometer needle was flickering at seventy miles an hour.

He took his foot deliberately off the accelerator and tried to get his behavior under control. But anticipation flickered in him unquenchably and no crudity that he voiced alone in the car could put it down.

"After all," he told himself calmly, "you have been laid before. I think."

"But not by her," he muttered, and rubbed his moist palm along his trouser leg.

He had two cups of coffee at the formica counter in the bus station. There was a trace of chicory in the blend, as though the custom had been diluted on its way north from Louisiana. It seemed another difference, a comment on change. Saluting this, he left a quarter tip and went out to examine the arrival board: King William, Gloucester, Saluda, Williamsburg, on time, due at four-fifty. Gate Two.

He took a seat in one of the two dozen pre-formed chairs in the center of the atrium. Hands on knees, poised, he stared out of Gate Two to the street beyond. It was too callow. He rose and ranged along the back wall, past the newsstand, the deserted ticket window, and passed away each minute.

There was a note of engine noise that was different and a gleam of high windshield that was not ordinary. There was a bus arriving that bore no resemblance to all the others on the road. It should have had cylindric shock absorbers behind its bumpers, wooden-spoked yellow wheels, and a roof rack.

She was there in the bus door and an aging, light-skinned Negro with a large basket on one arm was helping her down. She peered about for him through her sunglasses.

In the car on the way back to the inn, she was enthusiastic.

"It's another world," she told him. "Really, it was a marvelous ride. Did you see the man who helped me off the bus? His name is Fifield. Mr. Wesley Fifield. He's a retired houseman from Baltimore and he just bought a little house in Saluda. Where he grew up. He has two acres, some fruit trees, and" —she put a hand on his arm, suddenly smiling—"guess what was in the basket—that marvelous basket?"

Lovell shook his head, grinning.

"Couldn't possibly."

"Four piglets! Like babies! He had them all tucked up in cedar shavings. He got on in some little town up the line somewhere and he's taking them home. His nephew has a litter, he said. But he was so charming. He had this shy smile and he told me that the piglets would be 'the satisfaction of his old age.' Wasn't that marvelous?"

Lovell agreed.

"I said 'marvelous' three times, didn't I?"

"Four."

She took a cigarette from the package on the dashboard, lit it clumsily, and shook her head.

"Would you please tell me why I should be nervous?"

"For the same reason that I am. Suppose I'm impotent or something?"

"I suppose it has important connotations. But I keep thinking about the registration desk. The clerk, the people in the lobby, all the important things."

"I've been through all that. That's why I picked this place. It's not a problem."

"I know. I'm a fraud. It turns out that I'm about as sophisticated as I was when I bought my first bra. I bought it so casually that when I unwrapped it at home it turned out it was for a nursing mother."

"I think it's better this way. Seriously. And why not just try and get through the mechanics calmly and then the time belongs to us."

He covered her hand with his own.

"No matter. It's worth it. I know it."

She took off the scarf she had worn and opened the collar of her raincoat.

"And this ridiculous, goddamn outfit," she muttered. "Muffled up. I'm really ashamed of myself."

"How do you feel?"

"Seriously?"

"Absolutely."

"Very fortunate. Very happy. A little guilty."

"A little? Or a lot?"

"Mostly it seems to be uncaring. The only morality I give a good goddamn about now is that between you and me. Should I number off the things that do not matter at this point?"

"No. I just wanted to know if there was a lurking blackness somewhere."

"Gray. Like a puff of smoke. Very ephemeral. Very unreal."

"Then that's settled. But I'm glad you talked about it. I don't want to seem as though I'm compiling a guidebook to adultery, but I am cut off from other sources."

"Then we'll have to find our own way," he told her.

This exploration replaced the topics of conversation that

could not be discussed under their present circumstance. For Lovell it was an added pleasure, having as much importance as any other facet of their relationship.

They drew up before the inn in the twilight. He clicked the parking brake into position and turned to her, examining her face and expression for strain or disquiet. She kissed him lightly on the mouth.

"I could idle my way through the lobby and sit down on your lap near the fireplace with the dentoid molding. That's that."

She turned off her compunctions as one turns off a watertap with a firm and definite twist.

Having seen her to her door and been gratified by her pleasure in her room, he returned to his own for a shower and examined his face carefully afterward, wondering whether to shave. In fifteen minutes he was fully dressed again and sat down in the seldom-used armchair near his bed.

He cleaned his fingernails carefully and listened to the muffled movements beyond their connecting door.

He tried the doorknob once, stealthily. Locked.

He ordered a drink for himself and changed it to four drinks. He considered changing that to a bottle of champagne but rejected it almost immediately as inappropriate.

He stared out the window at the deepening twilight, at the shaped boxwoods in the garden below, and far beyond where the land sloped away toward the still bay to a point on the horizon where the last rays of the setting sun fell upon the water.

He saw two rectangles of light from Constance's windows and her shadow as she looked out, then a sudden dark as she drew the curtains.

His drinks arrived and were served on the coffee table near the fireplace. There were canapés and a silver salver of peanuts and potato chips. He raised this over his head and peered at the hallmark. Plate.

He sipped his drink and mused upon this scene that he had arranged.

He began to sort it out as he would sort statements in an affidavit for contravention or camouflage.

These arrangements: were they comic or only vulgar? A holy passion or a base lechery and a betrayal? Worthy or unworthy? Was there a difference between thought and act?

The sounds in the next room were infrequent. Tomorrow he could go to town and buy a stenographer's notebook and a box of pencils, leave the door to both rooms open and dictate loudly to Constance as she sat in an armchair, raincoat buttoned up to the neck. She could cover page after page with symbols and scratches.

And suppose she had nothing on under the raincoat, or only something? He licked his dry lips and choked upon his own imaginings.

Then the door was unlocked with a snap and Constance came in, paused for a moment, and came directly into his arms.

She took his drink from his hand, sipped it for a moment, and put it down.

"We don't need that," she told him. She drew him down upon the bed.

Afterward he lay staring up at the ceiling, almost anesthetized.

"I want to thank you very much," he said, "for your grasp of the situation."

She opened one eye and sighed.

"Just leave the money on my dresser," she said.

"If I could manage it, I'd be bankrupt in a week. What I meant was—"

"I know what you meant. Did you think I came down here

to run through the hall screaming 'rape!'? And I liked all your preparations. Your inn, your drinks before the fireplace, your lotions. You don't usually wear them, do you?"

"Nope."

She nodded.

"I came down here," she said quietly, "because I wanted to be wanted again. Not exercised. Understand? And I'm not making any personal comments. I'm not violating any unspoken rules. I'm here, my man, in the grip of passion, and I don't give a damn what's behind me, and I'm only a little frightened of what's ahead. . . . You?"

"Same."

"You don't make many speeches. Afraid you'll reveal too much? This is a privileged conversation—lawyer and client."

He found a cigarette and propped himself up on the pillows. She walked naked to the coffee table and sat down and helped herself to a drink.

"If I ever began to talk," he told her, "there wouldn't be time for anything else. You'd be seventy before we got back to bed again."

"Begin anyhow," she said. "Are you in love with me? And don't ask me to say so first. I asked first."

"I don't know. Especially now."

"Would you be able to answer if I hadn't grabbed you by your ears just now?"

"Better able," he said, enjoying his role.

"Do you mean to tell me that a little ordinary garden variety screw like that one upset your equilibrium? You must have been living like a eunuch."

He shook his head.

"Not like a eunuch. Chief of Special Services. You call, we deliver." He grinned. "As time and circumstance allow."

There was now a suspension of past experience. They were

like two pensioners on an atavistic holiday, displaying themselves to each other with a freedom remembered.

At eight-thirty she returned to her room to bathe and dress for dinner.

"Do you know," she told him as they entered the dining room, "why the Spaniards eat dinner at eleven?"

He nodded solemnly.

"I certainly do, and I respect them for inventing it."

They spent the night and part of the morning in Constance's room, their responses to each other sure and confident and they dawdled late over breakfast in his.

Today there was a chill in the air and a promise of rain as the day darkened into afternoon.

Then there was either a lapse or a surfeit, and a need to be alone for a time to assemble some approach to Sunday and departure.

That lay between them. Silently, they looked upon it.

At five they met for cocktails in the bar and sat near one of the windows, a hurricane lamp flickering before them.

They set about evading the past, and those seven in particular who were five hundred miles north and east who conspired against them.

"Let's get drunk," he said tentatively. "I don't like the set of your mouth right now."

She shook her head impatiently.

"Not me. I'll get drunk after I get back home. If I did it in this mood I'd start recalling pet names and clever little gifts and homemade birthday cards.

"I knew it was a mistake to get out of bed," she added grimly.

An intensity of feeling for her peaked and paled. He became angry at a situation that was so capable of solution, that they would not solve.

"Straight to hell with it," he said moodily. "I'm nothing but a goddamn bundle of appetites and desires. Every time one of them's satisfied I'm hot on the trail of another. When does anybody pass puberty?"

"Don't know," she told him. "I'm just the co-operative. And that doesn't make me feel any better either."

"I'm talking about me," he said, "not you."

"This is just exercise," she said, patting his hand reassuringly. "We'll leave it all behind when we go upstairs. We'll leave it on the table and when they pick up the cloth by the corners and take it away and shake it out it will go too."

"What about tomorrow afternoon at one, and then two, and it's time to leave? And you go to Piedmont Airlines and I drive back to Washington and take the shuttle?"

She sighed.

"I am so lucky, so fortunate to be with someone so optimistic. So bright, so oriented to the future. You are a pleasure!

"What I am going to do is believe that I visited Jean Marlette in Washington and that we had a marvelous time remembering our school days. Why not see if that works for you? You did go and visit your boat, didn't you?"

He grunted.

"Well, then you nailed up a chine or straightened a skeg or something. That's reasonable."

"I don't mind lying to everyone else in humanity," he told her, "but I'd just as soon not lie to myself—or you."

"You will," she said. "If you aren't now." She smiled with a trace of bitterness.

"So far," he told her, "everything has gone well. Fine, very fine."

She nodded her thanks.

"And so you bring up shit like that. Pretending this has never really happened. Not important to you, eh?"

"What? What's not important?"

"What we've done. Together." He gazed down upon the tabletop and smiled to himself.

"If all I wanted was a different screw, why wouldn't I just roll around in the back of your station wagon, or grab you at ten-thirty in your bedroom after your husband left? Did you think I wanted a little hole in corner ass-pinching?"

"Careful!"

There was a sharpness to both voice and face now, and he hesitated momentarily to pursue self-delusion and its importance.

"It seems to me," she told him with hauteur, "that I've endangered myself to a great extent already. And that the only way I can deal with someone like you is to pretend it never happened, to convince myself it never happened. I don't trust you."

Her face was flushed and she spoke rapidly so that what she said seemed diffuse and even pointless. He found himself coldly objective in rebuttal and the reduction of her argument.

Outpointed, she attacked accurately.

"You're like some old movie hero's idea of Byron," she told him, squirming forward in her chair and leaning low over the table. "You act and profess and caress, but you're too much, you depend on that too much. It isn't fair.

"Good God, it isn't! Voice it, for Christ's sake. If we aren't two dogs in a farmyard, tell me I'm your own life's passion, damn it, don't put your knuckles under my chin and look into my eyes! I can't read eyes! I can't understand head shakes! You're a liar!"

Tears appeared in her eyes and she shook her head and dislodged them, took out a handkerchief and wiped them away. No more appeared.

She glanced about her.

"I don't like this place," she said. "If there's a next time, we'll go to some trashy place near Times Square and take a room in the front that looks out on the top of the marquee. One of those tarred-over areas that's covered with dead paper cups that have been up there since World War II.

"Hurricane lamps and patterned silver! Spare me!"

From this rattle he plucked her description of the hotel, tested it for truth, accepted it, and used it to buttress his superiority.

Lovell had won a battle. But there was a sense of loss as well.

He thought of her partner in that hotel, a young Marine from Nebraska. With two hundred dollars in cash on him carefully separated against pickpockets. Eighty dollars in the shoe, thirty in the watchpocket, fifty in the billfold, the rest in ones and fives to make a conscious bulge in his trousers next to the other meaningful one.

"What are you thinking about?" she asked suddenly. "I should have told you how I can be ten kinds of bitch. But you really have seen me in action before."

He smiled graciously and she looked at him in fleeting disappointment.

"Oh well," she said finally, "if I didn't say things like 'aging movie hero,' who would know it was viper Constance who was here?

"I don't mean to be a viper. I was born believing, grew up believing, and yet I don't think I'll die believing."

"That's probably why we're here together," he told her. "It was a concept of ours, wasn't it?"

"You're so quick to go to past tenses."

"I don't think so," he said. "I'm just easily converted. Any proselyter comes along, boom, I'm gone. I'm with you. It never happened."

She rose to her feet and looked down at him, thrust out her hips suggestively and rubbed against the edge of the table.

"Fine," she said quietly. "Let's go up and let it not happen one more time. Maybe even twice."

They checked out earlier the next day than he had planned. The weather was still bad; a succession of black clouds marched upon the inn from the northeast. The temperature threatened ice.

Constance waited at the outer door for the car while Lovell paid the bill.

The clerk was as quietly cheering as ever and sprinkled his farewell with thanks.

He presented the receipted bill and a large white card.

"I wonder if we could ask a small favor of you, Mr. Lovell?" he said. "It's a questionnaire discussing our services. If you could find the time to fill it out for us, we would appreciate it so much. Or if you would rather take it home and mail it, there's a stamped, self-addressed envelope with it."

Lovell nodded and turned away. Beside the grandfather clock near the entrance to the dining room, Bailey Madden sat, staring in utter absorption at the pages of a Norfolk newspaper. Lovell glared at him as he turned toward the door but there was no sign of recognition from him or even of notice.

As he stood waiting with Constance he read the card:

"Thank you for visiting Great Inns of America. We hope that you will continue to give us the pleasure of serving you here, and at other Great Inns that we have developed throughout the United States.

"As you know, Great Inns do not advertise. We depend upon happenstance for our guests, feeling that such a chance meeting gives both guest and management satisfaction in our meeting.

"Great Inns are designed to fill a more subjective need than merely a place to stay; they are places dedicated to the spirit of the individual, not of the group. That is why each room is furnished differently from the others, why our linens and silver patterns are antique, why our staffs are selected for their interest in people and their feeling that competent service is an honor to both the servant and the served.

"Great Inns have no motto, no slogan, no statement of policy—simply the awareness that the Master of us all was also the Same Person who could wait upon His children.

"Would you be good enough to write a few lines on this card to give us your approval or your disapproval of the Great Inn at which you have stayed? The categories we set forth are merely a checklist for your convenience in recalling the points that you may wish to cover. Be as brief or as fulsome as you like. We shall read it with absorption.

"Your obedient servant: John Illingworth, Innkeeper."

"What are you reading?" Constance asked.

He handed it to her as she got into the car.

"Among your other attributes," he said, "you certainly have a feel for places."

"Children! The aged! Men and women! Work diligently, we beseech you! Follow the example of Our Leader a great and strong man who has dedicated himself to the limit of his strength to us and to our ultimate victory."

BOCA GRANDE 11 / 28

At four-thirty on the clear and frosty morning after Thanksgiving, Lovell went outside to wait for Max and Colleran. There was no sound to break the quiet, no breeze stirred the bare limbs of the trees that lined the silent street.

He heard the car before he could see the flicker of its headlights and was waiting on the curb when they pulled up.

Max had insisted on driving after he learned that Iacovino had flown down on Thanksgiving eve.

"He's taking advantage," he said disgustedly. "There's no reason for that."

He drove all the way himself, Colleran in the back seat asleep most of the way, and in a little over seven hours they were turning into Jensen's yard.

In the rigger's shed at the head of Jensen's main dock the crew for the day's trial had foregathered.

Jensen was there, and the young rigger, Halvorsen, Grant, the designer, dressed for sailing in a business suit, brown oxfords, and a black rubber raincoat against the possibility of spray in the cockpit, and Charlie Iacovino making himself at home with the buffet lunch that Jensen had provided: a locally smoked ham, head cheese, several different kinds of herrings and sardines, a couple of Norwegian cheeses flecked with caraway seeds, home-baked black bread, a huge blue enamelware pot of coffee, a small keg of beer, and a couple of bottles of iced akvavit that went from hand to hand.

"Eat all you can in twenty minutes, uh," Jensen said with a wave of his hand. He squinted at the sun and the sea. "Then we go sailing on your boat."

"Great night," Iacovino told them through a sandwich the size of three ordinary ones, "you guys should have been here. I met a broad who works for the Department of Agriculture and she screws like a Panamanian.

"Great food, huh? Like to take some of this bread along with us when we go south. It'd keep for a month."

"How does a Panamanian screw?" Colleran asked. "Like a Colombian or a Uruguayan?"

"Figure of speech," Iacovino answered and took a pull on one of the akvavit bottles. Max looked at him with distaste. He ate a bit of herring and was gratified when Jensen noticed.

"Raw fish for seafarers, uh, that's the sign of the sailor."

He was equally good with Colleran.

"In every crew there should be a professor, uh. So the rest can understand about the sea and the earth and the tides."

Nor did he forget Lovell.

"When you're ready, Captain," he said with apparent deference, "we get going."

The tide was falling and *Avatar* was well below dock level. But at a glance they saw a different boat.

She was decked over with fresh plywood—temporary, Halvorsen told them, until it was decided finally what her winch and deck layout would be. There were no lifelines, only flimsy bow and stern pulpits that Iacovino regarded without enthusiasm.

"No way, man," he said to Lovell before climbing down to deck level. "Not for somebody over a hundred and ten pounds."

"For today only," Jensen said. "I don't send anybody to sea like that, uh? Look at the foredeck. That's your office, uh?"

He pointed out the new arrangement of wire-rope that would raise and lower the inboard end of the spinnaker pole and its special winch; the fairings on the new mast spreaders; the forward hatch arrangement that would speed sail changes; the placement of the new vents.

The rest of *Avatar* also promised much and equally, at present, offered little. The four large sheet winches planted at the corners of the main cockpit were mounted on raw aluminum supports with edges still sharp from the machinist's bench. There was a new traveler for the main sheet aft of the cockpit but the stops were a couple of heavy machine bolts. There were painted lines everywhere on deck—two or three for the genoa tracks on both port and starboard sides and the lower section of the mast was covered with messages and warnings about mast wiring, downhauls, deck leads, reserved areas for fuel and water cap placement, and numerous arrows, including one all alone ten feet above the boom and marked simply "Up."

Jensen took the wheel, started the engine, and listened critically for a moment while Halvorsen cast off two lines and left them on the dock. Iacovino stood by the bowline and bawled, "Say when, Oley."

"Sigurd," Jensen said calmly, "that's the name, uh. And don't yell. I'm thirty feet away."

He nodded, Iacovino cast off, and with a delicate touch on throttle and wheel, Jensen eased *Avatar* out into the channel and away into the lowering day.

"Fuel injection diesel," he told the group assembled. "Light, but a lot of power, uh." *Avatar* increased her bow wave to the thrumming.

"Too much noise," Jensen said. "Check the shaft alignment."

Grant sat hunched against the cabin bulkhead, a small notebook on his lap, and made notes.

They rounded a buoy at the head of the cove and met the first small sea. Jensen's countenance brightened at the feel of it. He spread his feet a bit wider and smiled happily.

"Not bad, by God. She takes it right."

"Who's your helmsman, Captain?" he asked, and Lovell nodded at Colleran.

Jensen relinquished the wheel to him and gestured to Halvorsen to hank and set the new genoa. The genoa leads were set, the sheets rove, and Colleran put the bow into the wind until they hoisted the main and then the jib.

Past the headland the breeze rose to ten knots and more in an occasional puff, the sea was a short chop with an occasional whitecap. *Avatar* horsed up and down in uncomfortable jerks.

Jensen was impatient.

"Pay off now, get a tack, uh."

Colleran let her head fall off and found the breeze. The genoa luff tightened, the leech formed a full, solid curve, and *Avatar* moved, heeling to the breeze so suddenly that Iacovino's feet went out from under him and he slid helplessly down the lee side of the foredeck, startled, but making little of it when he recovered himself.

His ebullience vanished. He rejoined them all in the cockpit, letting Jensen and Halvorsen work the boat.

Watching them at it, easing and trimming the sheets, eying the placement of the leads, the lay of the blocks, the appearance of leech and luff, clew and roach, Lovell was aware of the vast differences that lay between them and *Avatar*'s crew.

The hitches that they made were the result of so many thrown; when they tailed a sheet they were always in the space that offered the best physical advantage; on a tack or a jibe there was a clearance between their heads and the boom—enough and no more, even over a lump of sea.

Artificers worked this way: cobblers, butchers, plumbers, plasterers who could finish a wall so that one might fresco it. But this is less common, and the more satisfying.

At one point, Max took an extra turn of the genoa sheet around the cleat where Jensen had hitched it. Jensen removed it forthwith.

He did not reprove. He merely grunted and removed it with two horn-skinned fingers.

"Not wanted. Not needed. Like tits on a bull."

Max smiled in embarrassment and squinted up at the masthead.

The backstay was now fitted with a new hydraulic tension-control device and Halvorsen took a strain on it.

"Mast has a twist at the top," he reported to Jensen, as they beat their way upwind.

Colleran nodded to Lovell and turned the wheel over to him.

The spokes were impersonal to his touch, but that was a small thing compared to the feel of the boat.

Whatever there was of the old *Avatar* had vanished. Somewhere below the grease-stained plywood there were beams and stringers that were the same, but the boat and its characteristics, its assured, plowing motion through the sea, had disappeared.

This boat moved birdlike across the surface, as though the

keel had fallen off. Jensen watched him closely and even Grant glanced up.

"Bad feel, uh?" Jensen said. "Not a good grip, kind of?"

Lovell nodded.

"If it doesn't get better," he said, "we'll change the name to *Anxiety*."

"Man, you can see it all over your face," Iacovino broke in. "It's a new boat. Be a little aggressive with it. Come on! Drive it!"

Colleran shook his head and grinned.

"Goddamn it, you got it," Lovell told him.

He spun the wheel hard over and not until the king spoke was a foot off the deck did he say, "Tacking!"

No sooner had they trimmed, three of them tossed together like sail bags in the cockpit, than he paid off downwind.

"Ease the sheets, ease them. Come on!"

They came down into a trough of sea and the next wave, small but with a carry to it, washed up under the abbreviated counter and rammed them ahead.

The wheel was free in his hand and he whipped it back and forth until he could feel the new rudder take hold.

The boat shuddered off upwind and he brought it back as one steers an overpowered car through an S-curve.

"Jesus Christ," Max gasped. "Take it easy. It was just a comment."

"Fuck him and his comments," Lovell said. He stole a glance over his shoulder at the next wave.

This one he seemed to take properly. Again *Avatar* lifted and drove ahead, but under control. This time the hull seemed to draw power from the crest.

He stayed there, learning, concentrating, feet spread wide, tense and oblivious of them, now missing narrowly, now by a large margin, but more frequently finding engagement.

He held on for fifteen minutes and then Jensen took over from him and smiled approval.

"You make a seaman," he said. "But I got to gentle this horse down, uh?"

"By the lee she would break all your backs. No matter what the goddamn computer says."

Grant had received a blow on the side of his head from Colleran's elbow. At least twice the others had stamped on his narrow-toed oxfords. He was not in the best of moods.

"You won't change anything," he told Jensen, "until we punch some changes into the tape. I have all the data I need, so you can go back anytime."

"Drive back," Jensen said.

"Whatever," Grant said. "The trouble with you people is now the future's here, you're just beginning to understand the past.

"Nobody could sell you a Cord automobile in its time, or enough Packards so that the company could survive. Now that they're all thirty years old you want them. This country discovers good design a generation late.

"Eventually, this boat," he said, tapping his pen upon his notebook, "will do what it's supposed to do, perform all its assigned functions better than what we started with. Except aesthetically maybe, which is nothing to me. But as a system it'll be better."

"In December then," Jensen told him. "Then we see, uh?"

The third week in December they returned again.

Carried away by the pre-Christmas spirit and his new affluence, Lovell rented a suite at the inn. The management reveled in the seasons. It festooned the public rooms, hung great holly wreaths at each of the milled doors, and set out Dickensian bounty on the hunt tables in the bar. Iacovino was not really happy there.

"No broads," he said glumly. "This place, everybody brings his own. I should've hired one in town. It's like on Eniwetok with me and these maids. Every day they look whiter."

Colleran shook his head in sympathy.

"Been here four hours already. How will you get through the night?"

"Find a whorehouse," Lovell said. "Here's my credit card."

"Laugh, go ahead," Iacovino said. "It's really difficult for me. Every time I see a hotel I get horny. Seriously. I think of all the time I'm wasting with that big room upstairs, two beds, a bottle. Umh!"

Outside, an icy north wind rattled the window.

Lovell listened to it with apprehension.

"When you get back here tomorrow night," he said, "you'll be glad to crawl in with a hot water bottle."

"And your hand," Max said, grinning.

They were out at seven and on Jensen's dock at eight. If anything, the wind had increased during the night. The cups of *Avatar*'s anemometer whirled madly at the masthead.

There was skim ice in the tidal pockets around the deserted shipways. Beyond the cove, line after line of low gray clouds, pale purple at the base, marched forward in endless, unlighted ranks.

Muffled in heavy sweaters and foul-weather suits, they hunched their shoulders and waited for Jensen.

"The joys of yachting," Colleran muttered.

"You're not having fun," Max said. "Tell me. You aren't having fun either."

Iacovino sat with his back against three pilings, out of the wind.

"Fuck off," he grunted.

"Listen," Max said, "we have a lot to be grateful for. Suppose that computerized designer had made a schooner with a square rig? A tea clipper or something.

"If that was what that tape of his called for, that's what you'd have, John. Or a Viking ship with square yards and cowhide shields down the gunwales. By God, that Jensen would have loved it.

"I can hear the son of a bitch now: 'I got to put in a bigger steering oar, uh. Ten more benches for the rowers, uh. All English oak, edge glued. A boat like that you could take to Iceland.' "

"Who in the hell would ever want to go to Iceland but a Norwegian?"

Jensen and his rigger appeared.

"I was here at six," he told them, "but Grant called. He won't be here today, uh. He's got a cold."

He led the way down the iron ladder. They followed, making an unwilling commitment to the day, accepting the experience as another series of discomforts in the march on accomplishment.

The engine did not start. Air lock in the fuel line, Jensen said, and cursed unintelligibly.

"Never mind," he said finally, and gestured to Halvorsen. "We sail her off."

They hanked on the heaviest genoa, hoisted the main, and stood by the deck lines. It was not a maneuver they would have attempted themselves in this gusting onshore breeze. There was the narrow channel to beat through; the haphazard pilings to avoid on every tack.

Jensen managed it, utilizing each perceptible drop in wind velocity. He stationed three of them with fenders bow, stern and amidship, and with Lovell and Halvorsen paying off and taking tension on the mooring lines he eased *Avatar* safely away from the dock, trimmed the main to capture just enough breeze for maneuver, and headed seaward unscathed.

Lovell and his crew were as pleased as though they had done it alone. So pleased that they pretended as one that this was the way they always put to sea: casually, confident in their own abilities.

Jensen ignored them, peering intently ahead to time the next tack, calculating wind, tide, and sea with utter precision. He headed off the wind to a close reach, turned the helm over to Colleran, and went below to examine the fuel lines to the diesel.

"Come on," Colleran said to Lovell as they moved offshore, "try her. She seems much easier now."

It was true. Even in these seas, *Avatar* moved with grace. Her steering was much improved. Lovell eased both sails and headed off into a broader reach. Jensen came on deck again, eyed the trim, and shook his head angrily.

"Now I got to put a gravity tank in that fuel system someplace, uh. Mr. Designer says we can't have no trouble with the engine. No trouble at all. In forty years I never saw an engine that didn't have trouble. With one cylinder you have a little trouble. Two, twice as much. You got four. If you don't want trouble, ship the mechanic from Detroit with the boat. When you open up this engine you will have a wave like a barge in a headwind. He won't tell you that, Mr. Designer, uh? I'll tell you.

"Harden up, goddamn it," he said to Lovell loudly. "Why do you go from one reach to another. Point this boat. See what she will do now. While I'm here! God knows how long I will be!"

He went forward on deck muttering and lay down along the weather rail in the bow to watch the set of the jib on the beat. Over the deckhouse Lovell could see his yellow hunting boots, his checked woolen shirt. With the sheets trimmed in, hard on the wind, *Avatar* took water over the bow with a crash that reverberated through the unfinished cabin. The seas were steeper, gray, challenging, icy cold on forehead and hands. Alone on the clean-swept foredeck, Jensen harangued the elements, the boat, the designer, and the crew.

"Take him a lifeline if he's going to stay up there," Lovell told Halvorsen. "Go on."

Halvorsen shrugged, took harness and line forward, and tapped Jensen on the shoulder. He looked at the proffered harness, and his face, already stung red by cold and spray, purpled.

He seized the harness and line and flung the mass toward the cockpit, rose to his feet, and shouted:

"You goddamn, you! Nobody tells me. I'm the one who tells, uh! Playboys, you. I don't need no harness to stay on a boat. You wear it back there!"

As he spoke a wave of a different proportion rose behind him, powerful and almost majestic, that would crest or break just at the chain plates.

Seeing it, Lovell bore off to hold its mass off the bow. It broke just behind *Avatar's* forefoot, the bow fell off farther into the chasm behind it, the whole boat slid away for what seemed to be minutes, driving away and down. Jensen lost his balance, slid on his stomach across the cabin top, under the foot of the jib between the leeward stanchions and into the heaving sea.

Momentarily, his right hand clasped a stanchion. Lovell saw him grip it as though frozen in space, then *Avatar* drove on at speed, lee rail buried to the chain plates. The desperate, hopeless grip weakened, lost, and Jensen was gone.

Just then, Colleran jerked the port life ring from its basket, dropped it, and remained where he was, eyes fixed unswervingly upon its yellow skin.

Lovell marked the heading and glanced at his watch, calculating, checking the speed as best he could.

They jibed smoothly and with no difficulty. Halvorsen went

calmly to the fantail, removing heavy weather jacket, trousers, and seaboots as though stripping for a shower.

"Don't go," Lovell shouted. "We'll never get two of you!"

He paused in his preparation and stared, halted. He pointed outward.

"I have to," he said. "I have to."

"You stand by with a boat hook! When we get to him, you go in. We'll all go in."

Downwind, they still made eight knots, passed the drifting life ring, and went on. Lovell counted the seconds, concentrating only on his calculations, haphazard as they were, waiting for Colleran's hail that someone else might share this responsibility.

"He's up," Colleran said, awe-struck, "right out of the water! Good God, to his waist! Now he's astern! Astern!"

Lovell spun the wheel to hold the boat downwind of the man, shutting off with absolute concentration the thought that he could not face now. If he had erred, if Colleran had lost that sighting, there would be no minuscule chance to pick Jensen from the sea.

Then they had him. Halvorsen floundered in the water beside him with a bowline and the others hauled him aboard, immobile except when, as it happened, the great limp weight of him shifted in their arms.

Face purpled, water streaming from his clothing, they managed him below while Lovell, like an automated figure, set the sheets again and made off toward their harbor.

"Halvorsen," he shouted. "Get up here!"

Halvorsen's face appeared in the hatchway, a white blur against the gray dark below.

"We're working on him," he said. "He's not conscious."

"Listen to me," Lovell said quietly. "If you want to see him live, get up here and pilot us back as quickly as you can.

You know the place and I don't. Let them treat him. You save the time."

He scrambled out and in fifteen minutes on Lovell's watch they raised the light at the mouth of the cove, conscious of the minutes passing, listening over the sound of sea and wind to the noises from below, muttered comments, long interludes of silence.

"I think he had a stroke," Halvorsen said at one point. "He had one before. Last fall. Some kind of attack. It made him angry at himself and the doctor. Once I saw him after quitting time in the office with a one-handed cutter. He put a big spring it it and he worked it with his right hand, trying to bring the strength back to it."

He fished the tool out of his pocket and tossed it on the cockpit seat.

"Here it is. It fell out of his pants down there. I can't do it myself but three times. He was up to ten."

Halvorsen went forward and dropped the genoa as they passed the harbor light; the breeze faded somewhat. They came down the channel swiftly, quietly. Concentrating as though officiating at a ceremony, Lovell rounded up a few feet off the A-frame and Halvorsen leaped ashore with a stern line, fastened it, and took off, sprinting up the bouncing floats toward the dock house, shouting as he went.

In twenty minutes there was a Coast Guard helicopter on hand and a local doctor. Halvorsen climbed in too.

It lifted off in the gray lowering afternoon, dipped in hesitation and whirled off to the community hospital across the harbor to the west.

They left *Avatar* as she lay and returned to the inn in silence.

They sat in the bar with a bottle of Bourbon on the table before them. Finally they came to speech, after many glances away from each other, in a strained, halting, ingenuous manner as though venturing into the center of an experience that was beyond their maturity.

Another presence, a child, a woman, or a comparative like the designer, might have helped them.

There being none, they approached the matter with reserve, a wariness, an awareness of their association in an event that brought unease and uncertainty.

"We did all we could and you all behaved damn well," Lovell said.

There was a grunt from Iacovino. Max and Colleran stared down into their glasses, the business of the bar unnoted behind them.

"What I can't get is the combination of circumstances," Colleran said. "The engine not working; the kind of wave action; going through the stanchions like a spear; no radio. Whoever saw a man shoot off a boat like that?"

"The harness," Max said, almost angrily. "What the hell was he proving by refusing to wear one? It was his own fault if anyone's."

They fell silent, satisfied to assign the responsibility for his death to the dead man, now becoming certain that he had eliminated himself and supporting each other with this conclusion.

"He might have made it," Lovell said. "We don't really know yet."

"A crock," Iacovino said. "Didn't you see that doctor sink that needle into his chest? Christ, he didn't even quiver. What was that, anyhow?"

"Caffeine, nitroglycerin, something to stimulate heart action," Max said.

"Maxie," Iacovino told him, sipping from his glass, "I'm glad you were there. I could never do that. What you did. Breathing into his mouth all that time. What'd it feel like? Cold, was he? I mean his lips."

Max gestured in deprecation.

"Had to be done."

Iacovino drank deeply.

"Not by me."

"Without you," Max said quietly, "we'd never have gotten him up over the side. He was a heavy man."

They acknowledged their contributions to the retrieval, making their way through the calamity, awarding to each a measure of approbation so that they might remain men and sailors.

They spoke of Lovell's quick and accurate calculations and his handling of the wheel, of Colleran's absolute concentration on Jensen's position in reference to the boat, again to Iacovino's strength and Max's emergency treatment.

They turned up detail after detail. There was enough credit for all but not enough to satisfy them.

And just as they had raised themselves almost to competence Halvorsen came in, still in his orange heavy-weather jacket.

"Over," he said. "Dead."

They pushed back their chairs and made room for him. He did not sit down until Lovell got up and put a hand on his elbow. Then he consented and Colleran poured him a large drink from their bottle.

They shook their heads and turned down the corners of their mouths as he drank.

"When did it happen?" Max asked him.

Halvorsen spoke rapidly, almost breathlessly.

"I don't know. They don't say. They want to open him up to find out. Mrs. Jensen said no. His daughter said no too and his brother. So there will be an inquest tomorrow and she asked if you would come."

"All of us?" Lovell asked. "I would think just me would be enough."

"All of us would be better," Colleran said. "What the hell, we all were there, why not?"

"Not me," Iacovino said. "I can't. I'll give you a statement or something. I just want to get the hell out of here before I decide to stop sailing forever."

Halvorsen looked up at him in surprise.

"Why would you do that?" he asked. "That's part of it too. I wouldn't stop rigging boats because of it—even yours."

"I'm more sensitive than I look," Iacovino said.

He stood up, finished his drink, and glanced at his watch.

"I can get a bus to Washington tonight, John, but I'll have to take a cab into town. You want me to pay for it and reimburse me later?"

Lovell took ten dollars from his billfold and handed it to him.

Iacovino took Halvorsen's hand and shook it punctiliously.

"I'm sorry," he said, and departed.

"Where's the wake?" Colleran asked.

"Ackley's," Halvorsen said. "He's the coroner too. But the family won't be there tonight."

"How is his wife?"

"Okay. Good. She stands up like a church steeple. Her father died at Trondheim and one brother too. So she knows this." He stood up abruptly.

"Thank you, sir. The inquest is at ten-thirty."

"Trondheim," Max said to himself. "That was how long ago—nineteen-forty or forty-one? She stands up like a church steeple. Probably she's the old deep-keel model. Mine would be on her way to the bank tonight to check over the insurance policies. She takes care of all the premiums, so they're all paid up."

He smiled mockingly.

"Eighty-five thousand dollars at eight per cent gives seven thousand a year—not bad.

"And if they all moved into the garage and rented the house? Phew, it overwhelms me. My oldest kid, for one, belongs in the garage—someplace with a concrete floor where you can use a pushbroom."

"You should have bought a barracks," Lovell said, grinning. Max brooded on, to the ends of his estate, fescuing, planting, trimming, bordering the green pasture that he would leave behind him.

"And best of all," he said finally, "all that's needed is Dad over the edge."

They went on to finish the bottle.

When they awoke the next morning the northerly had blown itself out. The day was clear and bright, the horizon limitless, the sky that primary blue that raises the spirits and brings aspiration to hand.

None of them felt the effects of the night's drinking. They ate an enormous breakfast and were outside Ackley's Funeral Home at nine-thirty.

Ackley's was done up Bristol fashion. Its boxwood hedges were trimmed in the shape of hulls. The shutters around the small windows of the single-story, gray-shingled house were a glossy black.

Before the door was a tall mast with gaff, also painted black. At its peak was a gilded ball, this crowned with the five-pointed star that is the chart symbol for true north.

"Not Viking," Colleran said, "but better than most."

Young Halvorsen was there, and his grandfather, and other men from the yard. The men grouped themselves together and the women did also, as though in agreement that this was an asocial convocation at which professional interests took precedence.

At ten twenty-five, the Jensen family appeared and sat together in the front row and at ten-thirty Coroner Ackley entered, clad in a double-breasted black suit cut like a navy officer's uniform but without insignia. He wore a decoration bar in his lapel.

He rapped for order and the low hum of conversation ceased immediately.

He read from a sheaf of papers.

"Inquiry into the death of Sigurd Jensen, resident of this township, before me in my capacity as coroner of this township of New Suffolk, concerning the reason for and responsibility for, if such be known, or can be discovered by those present at the time such death of Sigurd Jensen occurred."

He paused for breath. A young man seated across the stated aisle from the Jensens rose with his hand in the air.

Coroner Ackley looked down one side of the room, across it at the back, and forward again before he saw him.

"Mr. Ackley," he began.

"Coroner Ackley."

"Right. Coroner Ackley. I beg your pardon. My company is the holder of an insurance policy on the deceased's life, sir, and we would respectfully request that this inquest be postponed until the company can be represented by counsel."

"Why?"

"Because of the company's having written a policy on Sigurd Jensen, sir. I was only notified of his death this morning and I am not prepared to represent the company on a matter of this importance."

"This inquiry isn't concerned with the company, Herbert," Coroner Ackley said patiently. "We want to establish what I just read. Can we go on now?"

Herbert sat down. On the edge of his chair.

They went on in a neat and orderly manner that would have warmed any admiral's heart.

The coroner heard Jensen's yard foreman and carpenter and engine mechanic, and through them they established that *Avatar* was sound of hull and fitting. They called several other men who testified to Jensen's technical abilities.

They testified that yesterday's weather and winds were only enough to sharpen his sensitivities. It had been a perfect day to examine a boat thoroughly.

Halvorsen gave the details calmly and quietly as though reporting on the loss overside of a sack of wheat.

He told of the boat's reconstruction and of changes in hull form and configuration, implied that the sea had claimed another of its own because of a combination of circumstances.

"How long," Coroner Ackley asked, "was the deceased unsupported in the water?"

"I don't know exactly, your honor," Halvorsen said. "I only have my good watch and I didn't wear it on board."

"How long do you think?"

Halvorsen pursed his lips.

"Maybe seven or ten minutes altogether," he said. "Maybe more. Less."

"Getting him aboard?" the coroner prompted.

"Two more, maybe. I don't know. I was then in also."

The coroner nodded. "And getting him down into the cabin and so you could start treating him?"

Halvorsen shook his head.

Ackley rapped his gavel.

"I find the deceased met his death by misadventure, to wit, accidental death by drowning. The inquiry is closed."

Herbert rose again; so also did numbers of the spectators.

"But Mr. Ackley. Mr. Coroner. We have to have an autopsy. Jensen had a double indemnity policy. We have to pay out two hundred thousand dollars!"

"Services for the late Sigurd Jensen, resident of the township of New Suffolk, will be conducted from this place tomorrow morning at eleven. May he rest in peace. These proceedings are concluded."

The press about the Jensen family was too large for them. Lovell lead the way out into the sunshine.

"Just as well," Max said. "I wouldn't know whether to congratulate or commiserate."

"I'll write her a note when I get back," Lovell said. "Who knows—maybe she'll need a lawyer."

"Hardly," Colleran remarked. "She's doing fine without one." He slapped Max on the back.

"You ought to introduce Estelle to her, my boy. The two of them could start an estate-planning service."

They drove to the Jensen yard before returning home. *Avatar* rocked gently in the high sparkling tide where they had left her the day before.

Now she was properly moored. All lines were coiled, the deck and cockpit had been hosed down and swept clean, and the sails they had used had been folded and bagged and were back in the forepeak.

Taped to the king spoke of the wheel was a large rosette of black crepe.

"They have robbed us of every accomplishment. Fifty years before their invasion when our great doctor tried to tell them of his experiments and his solution, they mocked him! To this day they have not admitted that he was true conqueror of the fever!"

BOCA GRANDE 3/5

In Nassau, March is the antepenultimate month in number of tourists.

They make their first cautious reconnaissance around the square between Bay Street and the harbor.

They shop the hat stalls where straws of any color and trim, any size or shape, may be found, past the sugar-cane vendors and the beach-shoe peddlers. Then they penetrate to the liquor and china shops, the camera stores, the jewelry and woolen houses that line the shaded shopping lane until it is time to seek the next distraction—the beach or the gambling casino.

The square is quiet again—until the next liner, just now a blot on the horizon, lighters out its eager mass, three days out of New York and pale but encouraged.

Between times, the life of Nassau continues. The proprietors of some of the market stalls seize upon the opportunity to prepare a meal for themselves and their children, or to involve themselves in conversations about the day's business.

There is some soft laughter.

In late morning, before the blaze of afternoon, there is business activity on the higher levels too. Young blacks in business suits are back and forth from the post office, dispatching and retrieving mail and cables for the corporations that have established themselves here.

The climate is good for corporate progenesis, particularly for those businesses that are hindered by government restrictions in their homelands.

There are firms of substance and solidity that display bright copper plaques in the Nassau business district. There are even more whose names might inspire caution in an investor.

Potential Energies Development Properties, Ltd.; Mesology Research Corporation; Western Oceania Mining, Inc., and a number of others shared a small suite through an arcade above a flagstoned courtyard. A fountain played gracefully in the center of the cul-de-sac.

Several offices opened off the small reception room. In one, through an open door, Lovell saw a white and a younger but equally corpulent black in discussion.

". . . be so shocked," the white man said. "It's not very new. When you first came to work here, I told you, 'Always look in the barrels. Touch the collateral. Don't accept an inventory sheet that could have been typed in a hotel room the night before.'"

"Well," said the black, "it's depressing."

The white shook his head.

"Business. In business people take advantage of other people."

He smiled and tapped his forehead with his finger.

"This is part of your personal file, part of your experience.

The next time one of your clients makes an investment in a packaging plant in Spain or Chile, a bell will ring—and you'll look over the territory. You'll spend a thousand dollars of your client's money and you'll save him a hundred times that."

He riffled through a sheaf of papers.

"Now let's see what we can rescue out of this."

Perkinson came out of one of the other doors. He wore a white suit and his face and bald head were sunburned a blooming red. He shook Lovell's hand heartily.

"Good to see you," he said with sincere pleasure. "Come in."

They sat in two armchairs near the window. Perkinson poured coffee.

"Your boat was delivered last Thursday," Perkinson told him. "Too bad about the old fellow, Jensen. Shake you up, did it?"

"It shook everybody," Lovell told him.

Perkinson nodded sympathetically.

"Of course. It would. Two of them at least are quite sensitive, I imagine. Colleran and Berliner, is it?"

Lovell nodded.

"Not Iacovino."

"No," Perkinson agreed. "He's like our friend Madden. Fatalistic."

"And you," Lovell said.

"I thought you would be in a little better frame of mind," Perkinson told him with a wide smile.

"Here you are in Nassau—new boat, bright sun. Sparkling seas, adventure, competition. Absolutely lotophagic."

"If you say so," Lovell replied.

"Come on," Perkinson said jollily. "There's no certainty that you'll do anything more than race. Truly."

"When did you hear that?"

"Yesterday. We're a contingency."

He sipped his coffee and looked at Lovell perceptively.

"How did you leave your wife?" he asked suddenly.

"Nastily."

Perkinson nodded. "That's reasonable. Why don't you have her fly down and meet us? Maybe that would make her feel better. On us."

"She won't fly," Lovell told him. "Maybe I'll have someone else join me."

"Really," said Perkinson. "You surprise me. Who?"

"The woman Madden saw me with. Didn't you know? Was it your idea that he watch me?"

"It was their idea."

"Amat's also?"

Perkinson shrugged.

"He concurred. This operation is theirs. I supervise. I can recommend but I can't command.

"That could have been very distracting. Another difficulty that we didn't need. Kind of goatish of you, wouldn't you admit that?"

"Goatish? You did say 'goatish,' didn't you?"

Lovell looked out of the window away from this room and this opinion.

"I'm sorry," Perkinson said. "It was a needless complication. You owe us something and we can't have our schedule upset because you want to have an affair with your boss's wife.

"After all, we came to you and made our offer because of your stability and your experience.

"You should know better," he added in mild reproof.

"You're in an area that doesn't concern you. Not a bit."

"Not so," Perkinson said shortly. "You're bought but not paid for. There's nothing to argue about. That's the fact. I could have let Madden and Mat have this argument with you, but that would have wound up in a fight—and you aren't as young as you used to be. That's the way you came in here, looking for one, so try to be objective."

Lovell did, unwillingly, resisting, as though examining some physical change in a part of his body, in his respiration, pulse, or a pain behind the eyes.

"I can leave any time, you know," he said.

Perkinson allowed himself a little smile.

"Of course." He sat back in his chair and raised his cup to his lips and smiled at the brim of it.

"John," he said, "if we weren't old friends and I didn't like you, I'd sauce you over and let you believe that you have an out. But you don't.

"You might have had one if you hadn't let the three of us come on board last August, or if you had heard us out and sent us packing. It's too late now."

He held up his hand impatiently at Lovell's protest.

"Wait, let me finish. You've been had. Your strengths are your weaknesses. Your sense of an obligation. Your conditioning to pay for what you get. You are just not a free man. You think you are but you're really subject to your own discipline, tougher and harsher than we would use.

"Let me say this: I'm sorry to see you in this situation. I did think more of you. But, of course, I haven't seen you in twenty-five years. I've been dealing with other people in that time, and in the same way—same concepts, same treatment. Quiet, courteous, concerned. I thought you would reject us intuitively, no matter what, and if you didn't reject us immediately I was certain that you would before we hooked you."

He sighed and shook his head.

"But here you are, telling me that you go no further."

He leaned forward.

"Bullshit, John. Bullshit."

"You'll see," Lovell told him, his face flushing with anger.

"I'll see what? See you meeting your friends this afternoon at the plane and telling them that you've changed your mind? See you paying the bills from . . ."

He opened a manila file on the coffee table before him.

". . . Jensen's boatyard, Great Inns of America, Pan American Airways?"

He rattled off others: car rentals, winch and fitting manufacturers, rope and cordage houses, sailmakers, restaurants, marine goods suppliers.

"None paid yet and all placed in your name."

Perkinson rose and tossed the sheaf of bills back to the tabletop.

"What's that to us? A pimple on the ass of an elephant. What is it to you? Tell me. Will you moonlight? Go into bankruptcy? Ask your cuckold boss for a loan? That's most of your income for the next three years."

Perkinson pulled judiciously at his lower lip.

"Maybe you would. You might. You're quixotic enough, even at your age. It would appeal to the masochist in you to drown in that debt. That would be like you.

"But there's something that takes precedence with you. You're an honorable man according to you. Stupidly, blindly honorable. Actually you're a pretty corrupt fellow when you permit yourself to be: a liar, philanderer, false friend . . ."

He grinned and waved his hand.

"What have I left out? And coupled with that part of your character is what you imagine is you. Fellow who accepts his lot, makes his terms and sticks by them. His word is his bond. He'll fulfill an agreement to the limit of his strength. That's what I remembered about you, and that's why I came to you last August."

"I don't think you should depend on that," Lovell said thoughtfully.

"I'm quite devious sometimes."

He leaned back in his chair and clasped his fingers behind his head.

"I could sink her at sea, you know."

"If you can manage that with Madden and Mat and me on board, we deserve a bath. And let me give you some advice. Don't fool with Madden. There's no subtlety about him and no patience. It's his worst handicap but he makes it valuable."

"Any other advice?"

Perkinson shook his head.

"Nope. Just try not to let what I said bother you. This will probably turn out to be nothing but a training exercise, two weeks' vacation for all of us. All right?"

He smiled widely and offered his hand. Lovell accepted it and the warm handshake. Perkinson accompanied him to the outer door.

"Accommodations all right?"

"Fine," Lovell told him. "Just fine."

Outside, he paused at the side of the tiny fountain in the courtyard.

He could not recall a circumstance in which he had felt so alone. It was isolation so complex and complete as to induce a shaking in his knees. He sat down at the side of the fountain until this should pass.

From the office window above, Madden and Amat looked down at him sitting there in his navy blue blazer and gray flannels.

"The captain looks sunk," Madden said.

Perkinson sat at the coffee table, his back to both of them.

"The trouble with you, Bailey," Perkinson said quietly, "is that you were never in a panic. You've got a mind like a Table of Organization full of inked squares that lead neatly one to the other. That's another of your attributes besides the one you heard me tell Lovell. If you're lucky, that won't damage your career. If you're not, you'll die young."

"If I do," Madden said, "I'll have some consolation. I won't be growing old and gray and so wise that everything I do will take twice as much time as it should and be half as effective."

Amat grimaced with displeasure and walked away from the window to examine the shelves of lawbooks ranked along the walls.

"I'm not posturing, sir," Madden continued. "I believe in what I do. I'm not putting in time so I can raise roses and read Trollope."

Perkinson turned on him suddenly.

"Trollope would be wasted on you, Bailey. So would everything else I read except last month's efficiency ratings."

Madden glanced as though inadvertently at his watch.

"If there's nothing else," Perkinson said, "I'll send you a memo."

Amat sat down behind the desk. The high-backed chair was too big for him. When he sat back his feet were well above the carpet.

"Do you want to say something?" Perkinson asked coldly.

"I want to say many things. I don't know how."

"After thirty years," Perkinson said, turning to face him, "you ought to. Try, get on with it."

"One," Amat said. "Madden and I aren't equals, are we?"

"In the eyes of the Lord."

"I have reached my limit. I'm not going any further."

"Don't know," Perkinson muttered. "I told you, I'll make an assessment of both of you. Or don't you trust me to do that?"

"I do. I trust you more than anyone else. But I'm not even a hybrid."

"Right. You're not."

"If I were taller? Lighter? I am loyal. I have courage. I am clever, intuitive. Right?"

"Right to everything."

"And this situation is unfair in your judgment."

"Probably. But I think you suspected this all along—for years. You should have gone into politics in Kuala Lumpur.

"I am bitter sometimes myself."

"You," said Amat with quiet persistence, "can ascribe your frustration—to personality traits that are misplaced—"

"Overly considerate," Perkinson said. "Sensitive, empathetic —that sort of thing."

"But my major flaw is not to be American."

"A big one," Perkinson said. "Surgery won't help."

"It is no joke."

"True. It's an impasse. If it makes you feel any better, Mat," Perkinson told him, "the next Malay will go further. And so on."

"I spent almost thirty years chasing an illusion. You're as hypocritical as the British, the Dutch, the Portuguese, the Belgians."

"Not me. It wasn't I. It isn't I. Don't make that kind of statement. When we first worked together there was no more idea in your head of how you were going to spend your life than there was in mine. You didn't even become a citizen until twelve years ago. There are plenty of other men who haven't gotten exactly what they wanted. They come in all colors and sizes. You haven't done badly—"

"For a Malay," Amat broke in.

"You can be very exasperating. I don't mean it like that."

Amat was silent and Perkinson as well.

Amat gazed at his scrupulously clean fingernails and finally spoke again.

"I have a good apartment, six hundred dollars' worth of stereo. Orange carpeting. An American diet. A car.

"But I know what I don't have. That's what rankles. What I will never have. I spoke to a staff psychiatrist about it. He came to my house—he suggested it—and met Linda. We had been living together then for three years. She served a good dinner. Filipino chicken."

"Very good."

"Please," Mat said angrily. "That is exactly my point. He

observed us socially. We had a bottle of wine. Linda couldn't stand the whole idea. She was right.

"He was awful. Such a stupid man, with his perceptions. His talk about remaining a whole person, which was what we both were. He knew that."

Amat smiled grimly.

"And finally Linda took out a pouch and offered him a chew of betel. Those leaves had been in the pouch for eight years. I bought them when we were in Macao. It made us both sick. We laughed until the tears came. When he left he was still chewing and nodding and swallowing the juice. He didn't spit."

Perkinson laughed.

"You should have offered to shrink a head for him. Mat, let's leave this now. We have a lot to do."

Mat nodded.

"I know. But I have been a long time looking across the valley. The other side is where I want to be. Where I have to be. To be a man."

Perkinson sighed.

"I helped you so far, I'll help you further. But for the next two weeks we won't speak of it. Agreed?"

Amat nodded slowly.

"Agreed."

Rarely demonstrative, Perkinson got up and extended his hand. Amat, surprised, took it and shook it firmly.

His palm was pink like that of a macaque or a rhesus. Concerned, Perkinson spoke again.

"Just one more thing," he said. He paused to order his thought. Then Perkinson realized that whatever he could say would not help. Language mastery, adaptability, identification were not enough. He might say that. But how could he describe to Amat that faint but pervasive odor of the menial that one might remark in a white as of use but that upon him was an indelible mark that roused superiority in so many of his fellows.

"Never mind," Perkinson said finally. "I'd better do it myself."

The week preceding the annual Nassau to Jamaica race for auxiliary yachts had become in recent years a very trying one for the members, for the harbor master, for the launchmen, the dock master and his boys, and even the yacht club office personnel.

"In the old days," a former commodore stated, "I used to go to the outer buoy with a shotgun and fire it at fifteen hundred hours by my watch. 'Let's get on with it,' I'd say at fourteen five nine hours. And off they went, devil take the hindmost.

"Now it takes six hours just to get them off, what with starting lines measured by cable lengths and handicaps, so much around the waterline, so much around the bum.

"Bar isn't fit to drink in for days afterward. One of the bloody millionaires left a pound on a two-pound tab. In Accounts they say forty per cent of the bills are never collected. Get drunk and scrawl unheard-of bloody names and clubs that are in Kansas. Like to go there and use the privileges some bloody time."

There were other complaints: members' craft moved from moorings without consent; the naptha launch that belonged to Stiles hauled off to a public berth in the new marina, where someone had stolen the two-hundred-year-old brandy cask that he kept in the bow, and the turk's heads from the stanchions.

"Not Corinthian any more," the commodore sniffed. "Bunch of salesmen and manufacturers. Ought to call it the Nassau Boat Show and be done with it and start it from the bloody gas pumps."

But despite the grumbling there was a bright air about this club that lay in somnolence most of the year. They dressed ship every day on their flag mast and on their flag officers' vessels; there was fresh sand on the paths before the clubhouse; recent whitewash gleamed on rock borders and on every rail.

There was canned music all day until four, then strolling musicians until the dancing began after dinner.

There were arrivals daily and almost hourly of entries from as far away as California. There was even a campaigner or two from Australia.

Fortunately for Lovell's sense of adequacy, *Avatar*, having no racing record worthy of note in such an assemblage, was berthed almost alone at the new marina across the harbor from the yacht club.

It was suitable not only for him and his crew, but for Madden's purposes as well. He had a special radio installation to finish and other items to be brought on board that were not for display to the crews assembled.

There were just two other boats nearby that were entered. One was an aging wooden yawl that looked to Lovell to be marginal. He felt an immediate kinship with her owner when he saw her. She looked like *Avatar* before her transformation.

The other was an experimental hull of concrete and mesh sailed by her designer and builder. He was a young man of boundless confidence and absolutely no interest in any other boat in the fleet.

Just across the way lay all the others. Only after he had acquired some familiarity with them did they come to seem anything less than equally lean and powerful machines. First seen there was little to choose among them—they were an elite.

The skippers, mates, navigators, and crew members that he saw were also a breed apart.

Even if they did not actually bulk large in their colorful knitted shirts and faded and salt-stained shorts, they seemed to possess a breadth of shoulder and bicep that was extraordinary. Most impressive was their air of confidence—as though they had ridden with Ishmael on the lid of Queequeg's coffin.

If this atmosphere affected Lovell, Max and Colleran were even more awed.

"I don't think they put their pants on one leg at a time," Colleran said, peering across.

Max spent the first evening soaking his brand-new boat sneakers in saltwater to achieve at least that status as quickly as he could.

Iacovino alone moved among them as an equal with an easy and obscene familiarity.

By late afternoon of the day of his arrival he was lolling in the stern of a handsome yawl, drinking beer and recalling previous races in this boat.

By the time he returned to *Avatar* he was in excellent spirits and anticipating evening.

"You guys are welcome to come along," he told them, "but it wouldn't be any fun if you never sailed in *Kattegat.* Goddamn old hooker.

"Klaus—that's the owner—Klaus-Michael Werner, he looks like a U-boat commander. Acts like one too. When he came to the States he left the monocle behind, but all his crew are sure the Jews are going to grab him and smuggle him to Tel Aviv and try him.

"He's loaded with money—the boat was built for him and he ain't ever going to admit he's wrong, of course, so he built it out of wood—if he could buy wooden winches he'd buy them, the old bastard.

"Anyhow, he sleeps in a separate cabin in the stern—with sheets—sheets, I'll be goddamned. And he has a separate mess table and separate food.

"He runs it like an office—on deck at eight-thirty, off at five, and an hour for lunch. For him. Everybody else, navigator, mate, helmsmen, they're all crammed up forward in the pipe racks.

"The whole fleet is full of his graduates. He's like the German Naval Academy—he's got a nucleus that stays with him because they like his kind of discipline, but people are always leaving the minute they know which direction to turn a winch handle."

He laughed reminiscently.

"God couldn't shake him with the flood. The only thing that bothers him is if you drop an 'alien body' in the head. Then look out. To me an 'alien body' in the head was a German turd.

"And he talks about 'Kattie' like you," he pointed to Colleran, "would talk to a broad.

"Excuse me," he said suddenly, "that reminds me. I got to tap a kidney."

From below he continued to talk to them, a running commentary on the new cabin, its trim and layout, the bunk that he wanted for himself in the peak.

"Maxie," he shouted, "what a beautiful sea bag. And a lock on it. What are you carrying, a bag of diamonds?"

Colleran shook his head and grinned. Max shrugged and turned shoulders and hands into a twisting caricature.

"So listen," he told them, coming back on deck, "I know we've got a lot to do, but count on me tomorrow. I always go out the first night in port. Everybody does—permission to go ashore, Captain."

Lovell nodded, happy to be rid of him for the moment.

Iacovino saluted both him and the ensign.

"Besides," he said, "the rest of the crew ain't even on board yet. I wouldn't want to get too far ahead of them. They might think I was the boat boy."

He was gone. Rolling along the dock, waving to an occasional dock worker, and greeted finally at the marina gate by three others as like as he. They went off toward the town with never a backward glance.

"Real shipmate," Max said, dryly. "Salt of the earth."

"Come on," Colleran said. "He has some good points. I think he plays the concertina."

There was much to be done. They would all have to familiarize themselves with the boat's equipment, stores, tools, water, food, divide up their responsibilities, attend the meetings for skippers, helmsmen, navigators, listen to the special instructions from the race committee, study the course to be sailed, the charts, the light list, the tide tables, the meteorological forecasts, and make an attempt to integrate Perkinson, Madden, and Amat into the crew.

Lovell had made no specific plan to introduce them aboard. Colleran had asked about them, and Max, too, hoping transparently that he would not be sailing for days with three more like Iacovino, but Lovell had told them very little. Only that he had known two of them for years, that they were able and decent people, and that they knew something of the area in which the race would be sailed.

He had given them no details, and had even avoided mentioning their names.

Even if he had not accepted Perkinson's instructions to tell his friends nothing of *Avatar*'s assignment, he realized that he would not have done so by his own choice.

He had disguised his attitudes, his thinking, so carefully and for so long, and wished for what was now within his grasp for so long, that he was not able to tell them.

They were here, pulling out the white sail bags, with the new sails folded as only a sailmaker can fold them, the tacks and clews bright brass and almost unmarred by the strain of sheets, trying the mattresses, rocking the stove in its gimbals, opening the freezer, and pulling down the chart table.

Lovell sat in the cockpit and listened.

At the marina gate a taxi stopped, its roof rack piled with bags and bundles. Amat scrambled out first and began to unload, then Madden, a brown paper parcel under one arm.

Perkinson paid and stopped for a consultation at the dock office.

Lovell leaned forward and called below.

"Come on," he said. "The rest of the crew's here. Pipe them aboard."

It was not a happy meeting. Madden was supercilious. Amat behaved like a boat boy hoping to be sent on an errand. Perkinson's appearance was a disappointment.

His face was a fiery red from the week he had spent on the island, but it was obvious that he had not spent it on boats.

His arms and legs appeared to be spindly. His deck shoes were fresh from the box and worn with a pair of ankle-length green nylon socks. He carried a plastic suitcase.

But he did smile winningly as he came aboard and shook their hands deferentially—a deference that Max and Colleran knew that they deserved after a glance at them.

There was the bustle of getting their gear on board and stowed temporarily below.

But Madden was definite about who carried his impedimenta and no other could move with as much agility through the main hatch as Amat, so their attempts to help were either not accepted or too late.

After fifteen minutes of bustle there was a pause for direction and they all gathered in the cockpit and looked at Lovell expectantly. Madden had put up the chart table and was examining the radio equipment below.

"Well," Lovell told them, "the first order of business is to have a beer all around. One member of the crew—Charlie Iacovino—is on shore leave, so I think we can leave organizational matters until tomorrow and just use today to familiarize ourselves with stowage and equipment, informally.

"I've posted a schedule on the door of the reefer—it's not absolute, and if any of you have any suggestions, make them. You have seen the schedule and my letter about how we'll divide up the duties and the watch list."

The beer was served out and he raised the can.

"Happy ship," he said. They all drank dutifully.

"Tell me," Colleran said to Amat, "are you a Filipino?"

"Malay, actually," Mat told him with a wide smile. "Almost the same thing."

They all smiled and nodded in agreement.

Then Perkinson made an effort in turn, and Lovell, and Colleran again. But the going was too heavy. The smiles remained but the jaws ached.

If there was to be rapport, it would not be accomplished this day.

Madden took it all out of their hands.

"There are a couple of things I want to say, with your permission, Captain," he told them. "I'll be navigating, so I'll have the right-hand bunk aft, and all my personal gear will be stowed there.

"There won't be any equipment of any kind having to do with the boat there, so there's no reason for anybody to go in that stowage space. Okay?"

"What about the transmitter and receiver," Colleran asked, "when you're off watch or something?"

"If I need help, I'll ask for it," Madden said quietly. "We'll go over the receiver and transmitter, but nobody's to touch it or any instruments of mine without my permission. Okay?"

He looked at all in turn, and turned finally to Lovell.

"Okay, Captain?"

"Your prerogative," Lovell muttered shortly.

"One thing," Max said, reddening. "I'm studying navigation and I'd like to make sights. That won't bother you, will it?"

Madden shrugged.

"Go ahead. But I'm not a teacher and the position will be marked by me—only me."

"I'm not suggesting that I even help," Max said. "Hell, I'm not that good. I just—"

"I'm not trying to be a bastard or anything. I have the responsibility and I don't want to be distracted."

Lovell reached in his pocket and felt the keys to the ignition and the hatches. His hand closed around them. He gazed off across the bright harbor at a broad-beamed cruiser running slowly toward her berth.

Now was the time to take out the keys and drop them in Perkinson's lap.

Now was the time to decide, to turn the charade back upon them, to remove himself and his friends and to rescue from it the self-respect that was disappearing so rapidly.

"You just got a promotion to captain," he could say.

Perkinson watched him and Mat did also.

Over the arousal of his anger he heard Madden speaking; having realized how bad his judgment had been, he was larding them with fat.

"Hell," he was saying, "I sound like nobody I'd want to race with. But I'm not that bad. And I do want to go. As much as any of you.

"Give me another chance, Captain?"

Lovell nodded and drew his hand from his pocket, empty.

They spent two hours checking inventory that afternoon. It was Madden who forced his bulk into the forepeak to go over the anchors and chain, he who checked over the oil in the diesel tanks and the levels in the engine.

When they stopped at five-thirty he was the dirtiest—hands, T-shirt, shorts—but this inspired no friendship.

It seemed only a demonstration that there was nothing that he could not manage or would not do. It was a show of capability and did nothing to improve the confidence or the satisfaction of the crew.

"In the short time since we established our Democratic Republic which belongs to all of us, there have been one thousand eight hundred and forty-three incidents of naked aggression. Patiently we have restrained our wronged citizenry, but our patience is gone! We will live free and un-paralysed or we will respond!"

BOCA GRANDE 3 / 7

From that point, the regular crew was seldom alone.

Ashore, at the Farrington Arms, where they were staying two to a room, Amat or Madden or Perkinson was always there. But presences did little to forge that solidity, that satisfaction in each other's company that is a mark of a good crew.

It inspired only a vague discomfort, an awareness that their crew was not what it should be.

The room assignments were a case in point. Iacovino had demanded and received a room of his own long before they had come to Nassau. He had his own pursuits and Lovell could agree or not, he cared little. There was an open berth on *Kattegat* waiting for him.

Max and Frank Colleran, though, had each expected to

share a room with Lovell. They would certainly have not minded sharing a room with each other.

Max found himself with Madden, Colleran with Perkinson, and Amat and Lovell were in together.

Lovell had said as he handed out room keys that he hoped the two factions would get to know and like each other better during the three days preceding their start if they abided by this arrangement.

"Integration," Max remarked inadvertently with a thin smile, and then, conscious of Amat's presence, flushed at his own thoughtlessness.

They settled down to work on *Avatar*.

They stocked her, topped out fuel and water tanks, and went out to practice.

From ten to three they sailed in a medium but steady breeze over a bright, sparkling sea, running through the sail inventory, learning the sheets and fittings, adjusting the rigging for reach and run and hard on the wind, and lost themselves in the problem of drawing as much power from her as could be managed.

Perkinson was taken almost immediately by the beauty of the sport. He was clumsy but willing, and having been taught a specific task, never repeated a mistake. He worked well with Iacovino on the foredeck, accepting insults with tolerance, bagging and rebagging the sails as they were changed, scrambling up and down endlessly through the forehatch, snugging down the spinnaker pole and guys properly, keeping the halliards clear, and anticipating what would be needed with exactitude.

But Amat intrigued and charmed them. He was remarkably agile, deft, and strong, and he had a feel for the boat that was beyond any other in the crew.

From the first hour on board he took over the sail trim from Max, who gave up his prerogative in admiration. Lovell had set him to tack the big genoa with *Avatar* hard on the wind and he had carried the clew around as the helm went down at almost exactly the right moment, so that the tack was accomplished with a smoothness and efficiency that the other crewmen had managed only after days of practice.

Lovell thought it a fluke and put the boat about again and again, seven times in all. Amat was better each time. The sheet that Max cast off he held at the clew just long enough to ease the boat swiftly across the wind's eye before it was carried across the deck and sheeted home on the other tack.

He was as good at trimming the mainsail. Small, unobtrusive, snugged low in the cockpit, he tailed with sureness and competence and called with certainty for the tension he wanted from the assisting winch.

Watching Lovell and, alternatively, Colleran when they were at the helm, he learned quickly to check the masthead fly, the speed indicator, the breeze on the water, the condition of the seas before them when they were going to weather, aft when they were running, involving himself so deeply with the trim and motion of the boat that he heard selectively no conversation that did not have to do with it.

"Son of a bitch," Iacovino said admiringly as they sailed back toward their marina. "If the Malays ever challenge for the America Cup, you'll be one hell of a mate. Right, Max?"

He warmed to his subject, as always, with a heavy hand.

"When I first saw you I thought Lovell brought you for bilge boy. But you can sail with anybody. What are you doing on this tub?"

"It's my ancestors," Mat said, smiling. "Very good sailing people, like some of the islanders down here."

"That right?" said Iacovino. "I thought maybe you had some guinea blood in you. A little Vespucci. You like pasta?"

The passage and others like it were lost on Madden.

He disparaged by his presence. When he came on deck—

rarely, and only when they needed an extra hand to douse or to set the spinnaker, or for another complicated sail change—he made no commitment to anything more than the physical task that was set, and disappeared below as soon as it was finished.

Max made an attempt to discuss him with Perkinson as they sat together near the weather shrouds. He was teaching Perkinson how to call the set of the genoa.

"Keep your eye on the luff," Max told him. "There near the wire halfway up is where the sail luffs first. You say 'light' so John or Frank can hear you. If it's too full, that's harder for you to call. They can tell that better from the instruments and the course they make good.

"It's a bore, but it's a pleasant job in good weather. You'll only do it in light air."

And then:

"Bailey doesn't seem crazy about racing, does he? Seems to look down his nose a little."

Perkinson smiled.

"He's awfully good at his job, though."

"He looks like he'd rather be someplace else. You and Amat seem to be having a good time. I'm not prying, I just wonder why people do it if they don't enjoy it."

"Mmm," Perkinson nodded. "I know what you mean. An old guy married a young girl and took her on a cruise around the world. He went to a druggist and bought ten dozen condoms and a thousand dramamine tablets. And the druggist said, 'If it makes you so sick, why do you do it so often?' "

Max laughed dutifully.

"Call it now," he said.

There was a boat to windward of them, approximately their size and with the same rig. Seeing them, Colleran eased the helm a bit, in accordance with Perkinson's call, and *Avatar*'s speed inched up on the indicator.

The other boat responded with a seemingly casual hardening up of her jib sheets. Suddenly they were racing for the harbor buoy.

The breeze gusted up as they moved along to twelve and then to fifteen knots. *Avatar* heeled to it.

At the wheel, Colleran laughed and bent down as though in conversation to Amat.

"Trim," he said. "He's racing."

The other boat bore off and then lifted into a groove. They clung to each other, *Avatar*'s bow ahead of the other but a hundred yards to leeward.

They were caught up in the chase. Perkinson and Max stretched themselves along the rail, lying between deck and deckhouse, and Max pointed out the relative speed.

"Watch his bow," Max said. "If you see water going into it, he's moving faster. If it's coming out, we are."

Perkinson peered, staring hard for this indicator, and finally saw it. But the factor changed from moment to moment, as first one then the other gained advantage.

"Split with him," Max said to himself, "split."

The other boat was sailing lower than they were and Colleran said quietly, "Ready to tack."

"You roll across the cabin top," Max told Perkinson, "when the boom swings, and don't, for shit's sake, tangle the genoa sheets."

The breeze piped higher. Colleran stared straight ahead. Almost unseen, Amat came forward along the lee rail, sliding his hand up along the jib sheet.

Colleran spun the wheel and *Avatar* turned in a short, smooth arc. Amat handed the clew around and Max took it aft until it snapped full and Lovell and Iacovino winched and tailed it home.

Then they were headed for the other on what seemed to Perkinson to be a collision course, *Avatar*'s pulpit aimed like a ram, first at the bow of the other, then at the stern and below as the tack was completed, then again at her flaring mid-hull.

On they came, the seas having risen to an occasional crest, charging together, ten tons each, pounding across the distance between them.

The other boat held her starboard tack, her helmsman riveted to his wheel.

Someone in her crew bellowed "Starboard!" and was immediately silenced, disgraced.

"You won't make it, Frank," Lovell said steadily.

"Maybe not," Colleran said, but he moved the wheel only to hold his course and improve speed, not to change it.

"The race hasn't started yet," Iacovino told him idly, watching narrowly as they lunged ahead. Now they had passed the point at which they could fall back upon the same tack and let the other charge past.

Madden put his head out of the main hatch and stared, unbelieving, as the distance between the two hulls narrowed. Lovell pointed his finger upward at the other mast.

They would avoid collision, but he reminded Colleran with the gesture that, heeled over as both were, if the other masthead caught the *Avatar*'s backstay there would be no race for either.

Colleran glanced up once and nodded. He bore off and *Avatar* passed with a rush through the other's wake, her stern eight feet from *Avatar*'s windward rail.

As they passed below, Iacovino called through his cupped palms, "Did you say 'starboard'?"

"Come on," Colleran said, "cut it out. Is he going to tack?"

"After the helmsman changes his drawers, Tiger," Iacovino said, grinning.

They held their course to clear air and Colleran put her about again. Now the advantage was theirs.

They ate out to windward, slowly at first and then steadily, the spill from their sails interfering with the other's performance.

It was the other's turn to tack. Colleran sat down in the cockpit on the lee side.

"Why's he sitting down now?" Perkinson asked.

"Can't see under the jib if he's standing," Max told him. "Either that or so he won't survive if the bastard hits us."

Once more the gap closed between them and there was another shout from the other boat. This time from the helmsman, red with rage, frustration, or merely sunburn.

"Don't you balk me, you bastard," he bellowed. "Don't you pinch!"

"Also," Max said, as though lecturing in a classroom, "it's bad form to peer under the jib at his progress or peek anxiously around the headstay.

"Just wet your pants in your position while staring at and not seeing the set of the jib. That's your job."

"I don't know why you're taking these chances," Madden said, coming on deck.

"Get down," Lovell hissed at him, and he withdrew.

The sun gleamed brightly on the other boat's stem and pulpit. That was all that they could see of her. The genoa a full, brilliant white curve from lee rail to masthead obscured all of the rest of her except the helmsman, one crew and two horseshoe life rings. She came on, trying with a last effort to cross their bow.

Iacovino crouched, feet drawn up like some great foetus on the windward rail at the fore end of the cockpit, lips dry, teeth bared.

"Go astern, you fuckhead," he whispered. "Go below or eat bow."

Finally, she did, passing almost as close beneath as *Avatar* had, and the tension ran out of them as water from a bucket. The harbor buoy was almost abeam and they passed it and eased the sheets toward their marina. The breeze lightened inside the mole and Lovell took the helm while Colleran unkinked himself and the others came back to the cockpit.

"That," Perkinson said, "is what it's all about, I guess."

"No," Lovell told him, "but it'll do for phase one."

"How fast were we going?" Perkinson asked.

"Little over eight knots," Colleran told him.

"It seemed like two trains passing," Amat said. "I saw their deck stanchions flicking past and the winches and a face or two. A blur."

These two passages at arms rendered a vital service. However momentary, it was a shared experience that could be discussed and it opened other avenues to them. There was some common ground to utilize as a basis for other stories, for recollections, and four new ears for tales that Colleran and Max and Iacovino had made their own.

Madden remained unreachable.

Later he told Perkinson that it had been infantilism, a silly, aggressive action that had no meaning.

Perkinson disagreed.

"It does have meaning. You made up your mind that it didn't. In this operation it could be very important to you—if you get into difficulties.

"What's more," he added, with a reserved smile, "Amat understands it."

"What are you trying to do, get even with me? Set us against each other?" Madden asked angrily.

"I don't have to," Perkinson told him. "You set that up yourself. But I am going to do you a favor—you aren't that far ahead of him—and there's no rule that I have to approve either of you.

"Commitment isn't enough, Bailey. Loyalty, background. But the kind of work we do isn't managed from the top down. No one makes a commitment to you. They make it to ideas and to the men who express them. Trusted men."

"I'd rather trust your objectivity," Madden interrupted, "than your philosophy."

"Oh, for Christ's sake, Bailey," Perkinson said, halting on the hibiscus-bordered path, "listen to me! Have a sense of proportion. Don't think of yourself as 'helping' to take a society across thirty years of time. It's too tough for our department and all the other departments and governments. Expertness is gratifying, commitment is satisfying, but it's no solution. Sometimes the commitment and the expertness are badly used. They are!"

"What I do," Madden said simply, "is a comfort to me. Like a goddamn good sermon." He tapped himself on the chest. "Here there isn't any vacillation or indecision. I'm a tower in a sea of meanderers. What's needed is more of me and less of you.

"And another thing, Perk," he said, in what embodied more revelation than Perkinson had heard from him in two years, "my generation is led by groups. I looked around and I don't see the major figures—the leaders that yours had—individuals of stature and power. I've read about them, admired them. I was taken by them but I don't see them now."

"If there aren't any, maybe it's because they don't know how many there are like me. Or that they can't believe in me. Or that they aren't worthy of us. That's what I think.

"I believe in sacrifice, allegiance, determination. I take more satisfaction in that than I do in acceptance, fulfillment, peace.

"We're all making the same journey. I'm looking at the end of yours and I don't like what I see. Mine will be different."

They paused near the flagstaff that crowned a small promontory leading down to the dock areas. All about them bright flags, burgees, ensigns, and pennants extended in the late afternoon breeze.

Perkinson smiled at him, ruefully.

"I have an unfortunate manner," he said, "because I spent two years teaching.

"I patterned myself after one graybeard. Mild, unassuming, knowledgeable, calm, drenched in humility, behaving on principle—or so I thought. I imagine he did.

"I was sure that whatever your task or your role in life, that was the right way to behave.

"I have taken part in some strange operations and done some odd things. But I did what I did aping this man's mild behavior. Right? A kind of madness, considering what I was doing.

"Small arms instruction to Filipino farmers; teaching Order of Battle to Korean peasants; political organization in the Andes, as if I was a lecturer in humanism.

"Now when I look back from the present, when I'm always conscious that I've aged to the point of retirement, I'm not so, oh, how would you express it—upset or smitten about the way I spent thirty-two years so much as I am about my future.

"I've got little pains and aches that strike terror into me—more pains as I have fewer assignments.

"A moment of blankness in my head when I jumped down on the dock today—high blood pressure? Is my stomach pain an ulcer—or something worse? Why am I so preoccupied with mortality?

"This is what you come to. You're right, we're all making the same journey. You in a march, me in a stroll. And no one to guide us."

He turned and looked into Madden's eyes.

"Bon voyage, Bailey," he said.

The rest of the crew passed them as they spoke and, continuing, turned toward the veranda that ran the whole two-hundred-foot width of the Victorian clubhouse.

Colleran nodded at them as they passed.

"I hope Uncle Perk gives him a good talking to," he said. "Just so we get to listen to the radio awhile."

There was a long bar drawn up against the clubhouse wall, flanked by endless buffet tables, bright with flowers arranged by the club ladies. The whole was under simultaneous pressure from the visiting yachtsmen, older members who had forsaken their brass telescopes and left their rattan chairs for as many passes as they could manage, and from numberless officials in customs, tourism, public works, and transportation. This mass was extended again by numbers of women from the airline offices, the car rental agencies, the nightclubs in the town.

From this blur of faces—tanned, reddened, pale—Lovell, as he came up the path, was aware of three: Joyce and Constance and Ray Flickinger. They popped out of the mass like giants.

Smiling, smiling, they moved through the press toward him.

"Surprise," Joyce murmured and kissed him on the left ear.

"Surprise," Constance said and kissed him on the forehead.

"Surprised?" Ray said, shaking his hand heartily.

"I'm overwhelmed," he told them, and turned to introduce Amat and the rest. But they were gone somewhere in the milling mass.

"Here," Ray said, handing him a tumbler. "Martini. Saves waiting and battling."

"Isn't this the greatest?" He glanced appreciatively at a tall girl with long, pale blond hair. She smiled at him agreeably as she edged behind him.

"Yacht racing has its lighter moments," Joyce said.

"When did you get here?" Lovell asked, concentrating all his attention on the wonder of their appearance.

"This morning," Constance told him. "It's all Ray's doing. He told me last night and we went over to pick up Joyce, and that was the toughest part. Getting her to agree. But . . . we managed."

"What about the kids?" Lovell asked. "You didn't want to leave them?"

"Hell," Ray said, "we'll only be here the weekend. Back Sunday night. What are your plans, now? We don't want to interfere with them. We thought maybe dinner tonight, lunch tomorrow, and you're leaving when?"

"Day after. But we've got meetings and we have to be inspected."

Ray laughed.

"Inspected! For what? Rats in the liquor locker?"

"Safety, mostly. Life raft, the flares, radio, lifelines, cockpit drains. To be sure we're seaworthy."

"After the money you spent, if you're not seaworthy, forget it. Take it out and sink it. Off the Bahama Deep."

Having left these three behind him, as though they belonged to another captain, Lovell had no desire to see them here.

It would have satisfied him better to fall into the promise of the veranda, to rattle about sailing, to drink himself into euphoria, to find himself at the end of the night with a woman he had never met before.

But Ray was sensitive when he made any effort at generosity. He had already reacted to Lovell's mention of his schedule.

Two months from now, when the charges for the air tickets and restaurant meals arrived in the office, he would feel Lovell's lack of response. He would fulminate in small ways, rejecting a decision here, a suggestion there, and always with a witness. His kindnesses were paid for in some coin.

Lovell thought of the time he had been fired from his stockboy's job at a large department store. There was a small white card in the envelope: "Your presence is no longer required," it had read.

He wished that he had three of them to distribute at the moment to express his indifference to their presence.

Instead, he drank enough to subordinate the mood—enough

even to exchange what he felt were meaningful stares with Constance.

Then they went off to explore the island. They took a cab to the new hotel on Paradise Island. They ate a large, expensive, and tasteless dinner there in company with table after table of cheerless patrons who had drunk too little or too much, or were only moving their table silver about until it was time to visit the casino next door.

"Whatever possesses people to come to a place like this?" Constance said. "You might as well still be in New York. Look at the carpet."

Joyce nodded.

"Third Avenue and Fifty-sixth Street. And the drapes. I like that dowdy old yacht club better."

"I told you," Ray said, "the chef at Ville de Chantilly recommended it. Best cuisine on the island. He set it up."

"We should have come here when he did," Constance said. "The salad tastes like wet cardboard."

Also, the roast beef was an undistinguished gray, but the vegetables were bright with preservative, the beans almondine and the baby carrots gleamed like bad lithographs.

They fell back upon the wine, Joyce out of relief at having landed safely, Ray because the surprise was not well enough received and because the chef had betrayed him, and Constance and Lovell out of a need to be impersonally euphoric.

Lovell revolved his wineglass in the candlelight.

"A wine not brash and forward but gently insistent."

"Mildly aggressive like an aging lover," Constance added.

"Very funny," Ray said. "At sixteen dollars a bottle."

"Let's stay with it," Lovell said, forcing the empty into the serving bucket, bottom up. "Maybe the next one will have less saltpeter in it." He waved the waiter over and ordered another.

"Let it breathe a little," he suggested. "This one was gasping for air."

He pressed Ray with questions about the office until finally Ray swore in impatience.

"Christ," he said, "I didn't come down here to talk about the office. You've only been away two days! Nobody's replaced you. Who could, with the kind of mess your files are in? Do you have plans to do this every year?"

"Of course," Joyce said, smiling. "We're independently wealthy. We don't have to think about things like college tuition for two, or replacing the car next year, or taking a decent vacation together. We're going to campaign our 'yeacht.'

"What you do when you campaign a 'yeacht' is get together with six deadbeats and you give them food and liquor and transportation. You have them meet you in Nassau or San Francisco, or if you really want to have fun, in Rio for three days of parties and pick-ups, and then you sail away for a week or so, and when you wind up and you've spent all your savings, you get a piece of silver, maybe, to put on your mantel.

"You tell your friends about how the waves rolled and about how the girls rolled. Then you sit around at home for six weeks with a blank expression on your face and a controlled attitude as though you'd been tranquilized.

"You don't even fight, you sit there like a deck hand, waiting to go again, and don't bother me with trifles like your son is flunking three subjects out of four, sleeps half the day away and wears earphones the rest of the time, and your daughter is sharing your pills with you thinking you don't know how to count."

Lovell refilled her wineglass to the brim and sat back impassively.

She laughed.

"Not that you need the pills. The chances of becoming preggers by Onan are pretty goddamned slim."

She drank off half her wine and turned to him in challenge.

"Aren't they, Onan?"

"Why don't we go into the casino for a while, Joyce?" Ray said. "If you think you're so unlucky, you'll win a fortune. Come on."

For Ray anything would be an improvement over this hissing diatribe that promised more penetration than he wanted to see.

"I didn't want to come down here," Joyce said calmly. "Because I specifically was not asked to come. But you made the gesture, Ray, you and Stance, and I began to think that I was ungenerous and unkind and small—"

"Minded," Constance said quietly.

"Minded." She nodded. "And I thought that he obviously has a great need to do this, some desire that he's hidden away for so long and been the good husband and father. And I can't really stop him. He has closed himself off from me, and from you two—his best friends. I thought of asking you to talk to him all winter. But I knew he would just freeze up the way he does with me."

She reached down to the pocketbook at her feet, opened it, and took out a handkerchief.

Watching, Lovell saw the curve of her neck, the almost imperceptible fumbling of her fingers at the catch of the handbag. The beaded bag for evening that a smart saleswoman had chosen for him, with many assurances of its smartness.

Three hundred and fifty dollars.

Joyce saw him watching her. She replaced the bag, carefully, and turned to him.

Her voice trembled momentarily, then the tremolo vanished.

"No," she said, "I won't need the hankie. I'll be damned if I will. Ever. Not for anything that you can do to me."

She rose to her feet.

"Let's go, Ray," she said. "I've still got a hundred dollars left of my birthday money."

Lovell rose punctiliously and drew her chair back.

She looked at him and smiled.

"Thank you, sir, Admiral. I always liked your manners."

"There," Lovell heard himself say. "How could I have planned it better?"

"I don't have the stomach for any more of this," Constance said. "Don't presume."

"We have two hours," he told her, "that you can use to put me back on the right track. It won't put me back on that or any other track, but you couldn't be faulted."

"Don't be a bastard," she said.

"I'm not."

He smiled at her.

"Don't be so horrified. You've seen a man with the bark on. You know what all of us are made of. Remember how both of us looked in Virginia?"

She flushed a deep red and looked from under her brows at the tables nearby.

He put his hand on her thigh under the table.

She dug her nails into the back of it.

"You're either drunk or crazy," she said. "If you do that again I'll hit you right in the face. Right here."

"Then let's get out of here. Out in the semitropical moonlight."

"Never."

"Would you say I was devil-may-care, brash?"

"Nasty and disgusting would be closer. I never knew what you were until tonight."

"That's obvious," he said. "It wasn't Ray's idea to come down here. It was yours. You planted it. While you were brushing your hair, or in the tub: 'Why don't we take a long weekend sometime?'

"'Where do you want to go?'

"'Oh, I don't know. Someplace warm.'

"'Bermuda?'

"'Too cold.'

"'Nassau. John will be there. We could take Joyce.'

"'She won't go. She has a mad on or something!'

"'Don't be silly. I'll talk her into it.'

"And here you are. You were going to look at me guardedly. We'd dance. Sit on the beach together. Rub stomachs—which is all you're really good at. So you're still dipped in morality, but wet with frustration."

"Disgusting, disgusting, disgusting!"

"Honest, for once. Direct, for once. For Christ's sake, grow up and be a woman."

"You mean somebody else to step on."

She leaned toward him, her breathing rapid, searching for a defense, a false trail to run him off upon.

"That's a fine picture of you I just saw. Through the eyes of the woman who knows you best."

"I thought that was you."

"Don't speak of it. Don't dare speak of it. I can't stand to look at myself when I think of it."

"You accept that picture as the proper one, do you?"

"Certainly."

"You don't see any other? Pirate, sea rover maybe?"

"No."

"Then I've done well. Better than I thought. I presented the proper face to the world. I mooned at it properly and it's mooned back."

He leaned away from her in his chair. It seemed that he had been sitting there a long time. So long indeed that her hair should have grayed, her face become lined and sagging, her jaws fallen and working in soft movement against her tongue and gums.

"Listen a minute more," he said softly. "I'm not an unloved and unloving man. I have known times and lived minutes that had beauty and kindness and unselfish love in them. Don't you believe that of me?

"Most of all, can you say that I can't look for those things again except 'properly'? Suppose that means that I never enjoy them again. Is that right?"

"It's not for me to say," she told him primly.

"I know that," he said simply. He drew circles with the foot of his wineglass on the tablecloth.

"It's not your fault for not understanding me," he told her quietly. "My desire for you couldn't survive my faults and your blemishes. Probably.

"And besides, a feeling like mine is rare. As rare as great ugliness or great beauty."

Nothing in her expression revealed any emotion. There was no sign that he had touched her, wounded her, pleased her.

"I've never been so flattered," she said. She rose with that grace that he knew and went away toward the casino entrance.

He watched her walk away. He felt no alienation from her. Despite everything he had said, despite Joyce's clarity in describing her own dissatisfactions, despite Ray's dislike, he was still a part of their ménage. His tax form, his speech, his education, his job, all made him a life member in this society. He had passed from childhood down the aisles of approved behavior.

Just so.

He paid the enormous dinner check and returned to the marina.

*Avatar* lay snug at her finger pier, her mast towering up to the brightness of the stars. Somewhere in the harbor a small boat passed. So clear and still was the night that he could hear the thump of the cylinder as it plowed by and the wavelets from its wake as they touched upon the silent hulls around him.

Just outside the circle of light cast by the wired lamp at the end of this section of piers, an aged islander sat in a patched canvas chair. Three cane fishing poles were ranged along the pier side before him.

He sat and nodded in his chair. Each pole had a turn of monofilament to a dock cleat. When a pole rattled upon the dock he would rouse himself, take in whatever had hooked itself, drop the fish in a plastic pail, bait up, and sink back again into humped quiet.

Lovell had approached in silence and had not spoken, but the man was aware of him.

"I am always alert, sah," he said, speaking out into the harbor. "Watchman, sah, James Collins. Of St. Croix. I am alert to my responsibilities. My presence through the night hours has almost eliminated losses on boats berthed in this place."

One of the poles rattled and he removed what looked like a small eel from it and dropped it into his pail.

"God's seas are full of surprises, sah," he said. "One never knows what gift will appear." He laughed softly.

"My superior at the gate has told me one cannot tell the content of the bait pail from the content of the catch pail. But boiled up together one can make a nourishing stew. Very nourishing, especially if there is not too much care in the cleaning and scaling. And it passes the night away quickly.

"You have a very impressive boat there, sah. It is not a pretty boat, but it is impressive. You will be racing her?"

"Yes," Lovell told him, appreciating the liquidity of his speech. "Day after tomorrow."

"Fine weather with the breeze steady all the way to the Passage. It will be a pleasant voyage. I itch to go again myself as I did when a younger man and feared nought but God and my father."

He sighed. Another pole rattled, this time with a small skate-like creature that gave even Collins pause. Then he twisted it from the hook and dropped it into the pail.

"For spice, that one.

"But then again I am happy I am not a prisoner of the sea any more. Not enslaved by my old boat that called for a purse without bottom and time without end like a young woman.

"And not beguiled into chasing the sunset across the ocean or the clouds across the sky.

"I can see them just as well from here without splicing cable and patching canvas and scraping plank. There is almost as much to see in the forty-five-degree arc that my eyes look on as ever I saw that way."

In the darkness, outside his circle of light, Lovell nodded his agreement and turned away.

"Good night, sah," Collins said. "Sleep sound. I am here until late morning."

Lovell undressed and lay down in the double berth in the main cabin, staring up into the dark. Every so often a port or starboard running light gleamed red or green across the cabin top and disappeared again.

He slept and woke and slept again, concerned with where they had stored the covers for the cabin lights, the kerosene can, the spare rudder, the extra line, the sea anchor, and not with man or woman.

Then there was a white blur of a face in the cabin and he lay with his head raised three inches from his pillow and tried to make it out.

It was Joyce, carrying her shoes in one hand. He could smell the wine she had drunk and her perfume.

She peered at him, weaving a bit.

"Didn't you want me to come?" she said. "Didn't you?"

He could not answer. Such a gesture as this was beyond him. To approve it, to speak and to say so was actually beyond him.

He said nothing, but merely extended his arm along the head of the berth until she entered and turned her mouth to him, and then her known presence.

"Our Leader beseeches us, pleads with us, to stand as one great rank to continue our genuine revolution and make it a genuine achievement. All the generations to come after us will pay tribute to our courage and our strength."

BOCA GRANDE 3 / 9

The race committee did not reach them for inspection until almost one o'clock the next day—Wednesday—although their message, delivered by a dock boy in whites and a British sailor's cap with the name of the club on its roundabout ribbon, had mentioned 1045 hours.

Waiting suited them. All except Madden showed the effects of last night's activity. A smell of stale alcohol and cigarette butts clung to all of them. Perkinson's face was green under his sunburn, Max and Colleran when they moved at all did so like automatons, the motion of arm or hand moments behind the signal of the brain.

Even Amat showed traces of wantonness. His eyes were deeply and colorfully bloodshot.

Iacovino was the worst. He wore a large bandage taped

around his right ear, there were flecks of dried blood on jowl and neck, and the muscles in his forearms and thighs twitched as he sat in the cockpit, legs spread wide, and sipped a beer in painful, deliberate recollection.

"She almost bit off my fucking ear," he said, and lapsed into silence.

Max peered at him as though his voice were coming across a wide expanse of sea.

"Who?" he said. "That old one?"

Iacovino motioned him away with his hand, feebly.

"Don't shout, for Christ's sake. That's her husband's cabin cruiser right there."

He began in a monotone to detail the evening. The others, first hesitantly, and then with more definition, began also to puzzle out what they had done, where, and to whom, as much to restore their own faith in their memories as to impress each other.

"No, no," Colleran said to Max, "that was later, when we came out of the strip joint. I remember."

"You remember shit," Max told him. "You said you wanted to kiss a female foot and that she had the most beautiful toenails you had ever seen."

"Very ugly feet, I said. Her big toe on her right foot looked like a horse stepped on it. How the hell could I forget a toenail that looked like that?"

"Listen," Iacovino said to Colleran. "Listen, Father, what did you do with that three hundred dollars I gave you?"

"Me?" he said, his hand going to his trouser pocket. "You gave me three hundred dollars?"

"In twenties, fifteen twenties I handed you. Outside the casino, when I didn't know where I was going next. You remember I said that I might wind up in a whorehouse and I didn't want to take the roll."

Lovell laughed.

Iacovino insisted.

"I figured it would be safe with you, sure. You looked so sober. Like my good old Irish pastor. I figured you for two daiquiris and then bed. And you're a foot-kisser. A foot-kisser! Do me a favor. At least look for it. Maybe you put it in the coffee can in the galley. Where your mother used to keep hers."

"She was a sugar-bowl type," Colleran told him, reaching for his wallet. He opened it and examined the contents and glanced at Iacovino over it.

"Tell me the serial numbers," he said, "and I'll give it back to you."

"You're a witness, Maxie," Iacovino said. "You were sitting right there in the gutter with your head between your knees when I did it."

"Tell me the name of your pastor," Max said calmly, "and I'll give you three hundred more."

"I'll give you another three to stop talking," Perkinson said. He dropped a raw egg into the cup of beer he was holding, mixed it briefly with a fork, and drank it off in a single draught.

Max shuddered.

"Where were you all night, Captain?" Iacovino asked suddenly.

"Was that you on board here?" He laughed evilly. "You dog, when I passed by, the ship was rocking. Even my friend noticed it. Got her so hot, she had me unzipped right on the dock.

"You could see the masthead whipping back and forth like this."

He moved his forearm through a 180-degree arc.

"Whoop, whoop, whoop."

"My wife was on board last night," Lovell said dryly. "She got here yesterday."

Iacovino fell silent. Then he smiled sympathetically.

"I thought that was Joyce yesterday—and the Flickingers too, wasn't it?—at the yacht club," Colleran said.

Lovell nodded.

"They surprised me."

Iacovino grunted.

"Some surprise. I got a surprise like that from my father once. I was working for him—digging footings for foundations. For Christmas he gave me a new pair of rubber boots. Great."

Then they were silent. The inspecting group had arrived at the ferro-cement hull next to them, and they watched idly. The skipper gnawed at his knuckles and stared at them.

There were four inspectors, very British, very casual and polite.

They had decided not to approve in five minutes, but they idled about for another ten and smiled kindly all the while before they told him.

"Of course," their leader said, "if you can comply in twenty-four hours, we'll be glad to come and peep at her again. If not, I'm afraid you'll have to settle for a cruise around and about. Not bad that either, you know."

"I've got two years of my time and money tied up in this hull," the skipper said. "There's nothing you've got down here that she can't take, and you know it. I'll go without a certificate."

The Englishman shrugged.

"It's not my ocean," he said. "We find your entry unacceptable."

He turned and beckoned to the rest of his party and they came immediately to *Avatar*. Not until he went below with Lovell to look over anchor, chain, and spare warps in the forepeak did he mention the other boat.

"Must say," he said, "some of the chaps you send down here are only just bearable. Calculate the water they need to the drop, bend a rule until you can feel it ready to snap. Better off just to go and race their boats. Ought to be glad I'm not making the rules.

"I'd deny wharf space to eighty per cent of them. Last race a pair of them sailed right off their easternmost chart and didn't know it. Fine piece of work that was."

He stopped at Madden's chart table and looked at the equipment.

"Got a sextant as well as all the electronics, have you?" he said to Madden.

Bailey produced it in a handsome fitted wooden case, and the Englishman looked at it and shook his head.

"Doesn't have much mileage on it, it seems."

"I've worn out two others," Bailey told him with a smile. "Believe me."

"Never doubted it," he replied and, sighing, signed *Avatar*'s entry and led his group to the dock.

"Luck," he said.

"Pip, pip," Iacovino said. "Up the Queen and the Queen Mother."

"All set now, I guess," Perkinson said cheerily.

Lovell agreed. He set the watches according to previous plan: himself, Perkinson, and Amat on one; Max Berliner, Colleran, and Iacovino took the other. Madden, as navigator, stood no watches.

"While you're snoring, I'll be taking star sights," he told Iacovino. "I'll be awake twenty hours, especially after we pass Man Island Light. From there to Punta Maisi you have to watch your ass."

He brought out a chart and showed them what he had done. There were the danger bearings that might be needed, and possible courses marked out just far enough off the eastern side of the island chain to ensure enough room.

"Marvelous names," Colleran said, examining his work. "Eleuthera, Rum Cay. Crooked Island, Mira Por Vos Passage."

"Betsy Bay," Max said. "And Abraham's Bay right next to it."

They seemed already to be away on the sea. Each in his own way swept into these charts, these place names that they had never seen before, each poised to begin a personal voyage.

In the twenty-four hours before the start they worked in harmony to prepare themselves and the boat.

Next morning they were ready, knowledgeable about what they carried, what they would eat and when they would eat it, what hours they would work and what they would be looking for day and night to check their course, the sail numbers and the hulls and rigs with which they would be competing.

All of them slept aboard that night except Lovell and Madden. The others were out for dinner and back before the sun had truly set.

Madden and Lovell parted at the taxi stand near the dock, each so preoccupied that they were more captain and cruise passenger than shipmates.

He telephoned Joyce's room from the lobby and she answered as though she had been waiting.

"Well," she told him coolly, "I'm glad you're keeping in touch, anyway."

"I know," he said. "You don't have to tell me. Shall I come up, or do you want to have a drink down here?"

"I think I'd rather come down. I'll just phone Stance and Ray."

"Fuck Stance and Ray," he said angrily. A man at the next phone glanced at him out of the corner of his eye. "They'll manage to find you. I've had enough onlookers for a while."

"Five minutes," she said.

It was her usual five minutes that grew to ten and finally twenty before she joined him in the bar, as though to surrender the prerogative was to give up her marriage.

He told her so.

She sighed and shook her head equably.

"I was always fond of omens, you know that," she told him.

She touched the scarf that she wore at her throat.

"I know you don't remember it, but I was wearing this the day we launched *Avatar*. You couldn't remember whether you'd closed the intake valve in the head."

She looked back into the distance, hazy and unclear; colorful and chaotic, the distance that they had come together.

"When I went to the hospital to have Nancy, I made them take the same route to my room that they had when I had Jack."

She went on, like a sorceress, conjuring up images. These in their turn vivified his own until the head of his just-born son, blotched and misshaped, his daughter's hands, Joyce's exhaustion, an infinity of banked memories appeared.

"I would like you to stop," he said deliberately. And she did, knowing what she had done.

"You do it very well," he told her. "All I question is what meaning does it all have? You're using these things, but not as you should."

He pointed to a section of crumbling battlement across the bay from where they sat.

"What are you trying to repair—that thing? It's too far gone and it has no purpose any more. No aesthetic either. Some beauty when the sun is setting and gleams on a stone here and there."

He shrugged.

"Is it worth it to you? If it is, why is it?"

"You're better at this than I am," she said, interrupting.

"The one who asks the question is always better off. I don't have an answer. Maybe you're right. I did take advantage of you. Admitting it doesn't make me generous suddenly. I'm just what I was.

"I don't know why I do it. Because of my sister and her three marriages? Because I can't accept failure and shouldn't have to because you're not exceptional enough to fail with?"

He laughed at her.

"I'm not trying to be mean," she said. "I'm searching myself."

He cupped her face in his hands and leaned across the table to her in a curiously youthful way.

He kissed her gently on the forehead and on the lips.

"Good-bye, heart," he said softly. "I've got to go."

She put a hand on his sleeve as he rose.

"You know," she said, "I told Stance about last night—you know, when I went down to see you. Do you know what she said? She said getting laid was half the battle."

"She must know," Lovell replied.

There was a final ceremony at the yacht club before the start.

At noon precisely, the crews assembled on the lawn before the entrance for a formal godspeed.

There were some speeches full of bonhomie and restrained tributes to the hardiness and courage of the participants. On this blazing bright and unremarkable day it was difficult to dwell on darkling skies and tossing seas. At the very last there was an intercession with the God of all. The clergyman had a narrow face and a deep and throaty voice. He was determined to leave his hearers with an awareness of life's eternal mystique as exemplified by the play of winds and tides across the surface of this tiny planet that drifted through the cosmos with only the Divine Scheme to guide it.

He quoted only the theists who had lived after the Reformation and included as a gesture to the many Americans at hand a line from Father Mapple.

Then he sent them down to the sea in ships. There were two English hymns and, for the sake of international good will, The Navy Hymn.

All who knew the words backed their chins down between their collar bones and sang with feeling.

Colleran enjoyed it hugely.

"Crossing the T at Jutland," he said. "Off to meet the *Bismarck.*"

At the last note they were off like children, laughing, running lightly across the lawns in the sunlight to the waiting launches and the docks; here and there among them one or two paced slowly and with dignity as was proper for sea captains.

Lovell found himself beside the master of *Kattegat.* He was dressed in a double-breasted blazer brilliantly buttoned with massive polished brass coins. There was black silk braid in frogs far up each sleeve.

He nodded shortly to Lovell and indicated the disorderly covey of racers sourly.

"Four days out and they won't run so fast. Or yell so loud. They'll be sailors then, not schoolboys."

"*Kattegat!*" he shouted suddenly over the noise. "Stay together!"

"Good luck," Lovell told him.

"Good racing," he said, and made his way in splendid calm down the gangway to the launch pickup.

*Avatar* was ready when Lovell arrived at the pier. Colleran took the wheel and started the engine. The others stood by her mooring lines. Max was on the dock amidships, ready to walk her down and turn her, Perkinson at the bow, Amat in the stern, and Iacovino at the port shrouds waiting to lend a hand.

Colleran was waving in impatience.

Lovell took the wheel.

"Where's Madden? Goddamn!" he said.

"A minute," Perkinson told him. "There he comes now."

He was running, a narrow suitcase in one hand.

He leaped on board, flushed and panting.

"The man from Chicago," Lovell said angrily, and waved him below.

He eased the engine astern and they idled slowly away,

turned with precision into the channel, and fell into line in the procession that now passed from moorings and marinas to seaward.

There were horns and sirens from every hand, whistles, booming basses from the passenger liners lying just in the roadstead beyond the mole, ship's bells, hand-held fog signals, and cheers as the first mainsail went up on a seventy-foot yawl. She was scratch boat and careful of her prerogatives.

Off the harbor light there was a new breeze, a following breeze to the starting area. Some of the entries set spinnakers with impressive efficiency. They boomed out in bright controlled curves from mastheads to beyond their bows. Here was a red ace of hearts on a white field; there, brilliant random patches of purple and blue, orange and black.

There were others—bright blood reds and greens that vibrated madly when they juxtaposed with the daffodil yellows and wines and ceruleans of others.

They did not set theirs, to Iacovino's annoyance, but sailed out primly, shaking out the number two genoa for the start.

"You'll see enough of spinnakers once we round the first mark," Lovell said. He called to Madden to log their departure time.

He turned the wheel over to Colleran for the two-mile run to the starting flag and the hundred-foot committee boat, its flag hoists manned by white-uniformed sailors.

Off her impressive stern, around her bows, and clustered by the dozens in and about the starting area there bobbed an irregular armada in ceaseless movement.

There were sailfish and sunfish and surfboards, punts, prams, rowing skiffs that had been brought over from beaches at Bournemouth and Eastbourne. There were canoes, small outboards, open sport fishermen, polished plastic ski boats, native sailing craft with outriggers, and a squadron of cabin cruisers and motor sailers rigged with stern ladders and girls in handkerchiefs and sunglasses.

Max was aghast.

"Marvelous," he said. "What a drowning party."

They posted three lookouts and, reaching the starting buoy, passed it and turned up the line toward the committee boat, where early arriving entrants now were running the line on the starboard tack, having evaded the masses of spectator craft.

"Thirty-five minutes for us," Colleran said. "Let's get out of here before we kill somebody."

They maneuvered to escape and avoid. Safely above the course, they watched and listened as the water along the starting line boiled.

Those yachts under spinnaker arrived swiftly—so swiftly that they were upon the spectator fleet before either group had given any consideration to the convergence. There began a series of horrendous confrontations, salted with screams and obscenities. The racing yachts had sheets and sails to tend and little room to maneuver. The small boats were low in the water and unable to catch a breeze in unsettled air that was now heavy with gas fumes. They seemed in some cases to commit themselves to the fates as the entries bore down on every point of sailing.

The rage on board both sets of vessels was never proportionate to size or length.

The master of a kayak rigged with a fore and a mizzen sail was seen to rise and shriek, fist upraised, at a tall sloop that had not even seen his boat until it was left unprotected by a cruiser that revved itself away and left him exposed.

Two yachts forced to pass each other close aboard because of the press left a sailing dinghy miraculously untouched between them. The dinghy sailor, an elderly man in white shirt and trousers and a club tie, shook his head in wry disappointment.

Lovell watched him through his binoculars, unable to understand the facial expression. Could it have been disappointment that they had not passed closer? But if they had, his brightwork dinghy would have been mashed to scattered planking.

Minute after minute ticked away and finally, by means of bull-horned threats, short charges toward their sterns, and attached lines, the starting area was cleared of onlookers by a number of official launches that harried the mass like so many sheepdogs.

The sea along the starting line fell quieter of the numberless crossed wakes, the breeze rose to ten and over. The Class A boats sorted themselves into a competitive fleet and prepared to start.

"Committee boat end is favored," Iacovino called, "right, Mr. Navigator?"

Madden nodded coolly.

"Right. Course after the start is zero-six-zero. I'll give you a course change in about twenty minutes after that. Maybe."

As always occurred in this starting frenzy, Lovell, and even the inexperienced ones, became so involved in the complexity of the business that all influences that were not directly concerned with the management of this action vanished.

There was only the necessity to put their boat on the line as close to the lead as possible, to steer it with the utmost precision into immediate contention, to balance the demands of the rules, the weight of the breeze, the lump of the sea, and the pressure of the competition so that they might have a share of accomplishment, an ephemeral satisfaction with the beginning.

The start is both basic and sophisticated, physically testing and emotionally exhausting.

Despite the distance that stretched before them to the finish line days away—the finish line that they would probably cross in the dark and alone—they set themselves to win a test that had only a small advantage for the winner, but it was an important part of why they had come.

The brass cannon on the bow of the committee boat fired for the third time. Sixteen boats crossed the starting line as though fastened together in an artist's eye. On *Avatar* they began to count to their own start.

Fifteen minutes later the Class B boats left, Colleran watching the set of the breeze on both ends of the line and estimating as best he could the speeds of both windward and leeward starters in that group.

At five minutes to the gun they were high of the course, far beyond the stake boat. Max peered back and glanced at Colleran and muttered to himself at the distance.

Colleran ignored him.

Not until two and a half minutes did he turn. They reached back toward the fleet, inching low enough of the stern of the committee boat so that once far enough past it they could harden up on the line.

One minute, and their competitors, scattered heretofore over a half mile of ocean, were all closing the line as though sucked into a funnel, some on port tack far to their left, some leeward and behind, one or two hard on the wind already and pounding toward the center of the start, grimly determined to hold course and sail setting.

"Engineers," Iacovino called them. They came on as though on rails.

Colleran put *Avatar* past the stern of the committee boat, so close that even Madden gasped, so close that Perkinson thought he could have picked a gin and tonic from the hand of one of the men in a wicker chair on the fantail.

"Watch the white flag on her rail," Colleran told Amat, who

was braced high in the stern. "Tell me if I'm over before the gun."

"Ten," Lovell told him, and continued to count down. There was a boat below them as they bore off down the line—just far enough below to have no luffing rights.

Colleran put the bow on that line that was like a cable in his mind, and held it there through the turbulence of the wakes ahead of them, moving *Avatar* at such speed that they were climbing up on the yacht ahead like a runner approaching another's heels.

Farther ahead still, as Colleran headed up suddenly to kill their way and fell down again, there was a tangle. Two yachts moving like racehorses coming to a wire were attempting to resist and respond to a luff from a third boat. The windward boat was sailed as though alone on the sea. Her helmsman stared only ahead as though hypnotized.

The yacht in the middle suddenly gave up the struggle. Someone freed the genoa sheet. Her mast and hull popped straight up.

Her attacker to leeward struck her with her quarter, the windward yacht hit her again almost simultaneously with a noise like a steel maul on an oak door.

Immediately, the gun sounded. They were off. Colleran's hands trembled slightly upon the wheel as they came up to the best windward position they could hold.

Released from the tautness and the strain, Perkinson and Max slid down, suddenly freed from their positions high on the windward rail.

It was moments before anyone spoke.

Max raised his head and looked at the competition. Already they had begun to scatter over the sea, some clinging to the rhumb line to the turning mark twelve miles to the east, some caught in the wind shadows of others that led them tacking toward shore, some heading off the breeze to satisfy hull shape or helmsman's skill.

There was a yawl just astern of them, one of the survivors of the tangle at the starting line. Seemingly affected by that, she fell farther back, as though dispirited. Two crew members were haranguing the helmsman as he sailed.

"Frank," Max said, "you won the first award. The bronze balls."

Colleran grinned.

"My assistant will pass among you with a hat," he said.

"Teatime," Iacovino shouted. "And a rum for the man at the wheel."

Perkinson went below to light the stove, stretching his cramped arms as he went, and Amat came back to the cockpit to take the sheet winch and trim.

"You know," Max said, "as many times as you do this, it always affects you the same goddamn way. I have been through those rules a thousand times—ten thousand times. I can spit them back at you like a recording. But I cannot remember what I'm doing on the line. It must take a mentality or something."

"Maybe it's an evasion of responsibility," Lovell said. "Not an evasion so much as unwillingness to accept it."

"Shit," Colleran said, expansively. "You're making too much of a gambling situation. If you come off well—perform well—there's exhilaration. It's an ego trip—a big one. Sixty thousand dollars' worth of boat, maybe even a life or two—that's possible, I suppose. All within a framework that you bend to your own needs. You can always bug out or off at the last minute—or never even get into an aggressive pattern to begin with, and still defend yourself. You get a shitty start, but even the good ones do that sometimes."

"It's one of the few things I'm sorry that I can't do," Max said moodily.

"Lucky man," Frank told him.

Madden took the binoculars and went forward to the bow, a stopwatch around his neck, and glassed the horizon to the east and south of their course.

At four they began their watch-keeping, settling into the anachronistic routine that is another satisfaction. They tended their ship, watch on watch, sails, hull, fittings, instruments, applying themselves these first days with rare concentration.

The error on the helm was least now, the trim of the sails and even the positioning of their weight were matters of concern.

There was so much simple beauty in this race, such a sense of independence from the land and their relationships on it that their microcosm became the only reality.

There was nothing before them but the sea seen in every shade of blue from turquoise to cerulean to cobalt, presented to them together with a contrasting tumble of eternal white foam from beneath their ship's bow.

There were also the gift of sunset, the rise of the first stars in the heavens, the paling of the moon at the edge of the full sails, and finally the new brilliance of the dawn.

They felt keenly those sensual pleasures that satisfy because of their simplicity.

The smell of coffee in the morning; their bacon frying; their soups and their stews; their beer and an occasional whiskey; their hot tea and bouillon in the night watches; their rest in the bunks with the sound of the sea rushing past like an insistent hushing in the ear of a drowsing infant.

The idyll ended at noon on Saturday.

They were all on deck, idling away the time before lunch, on the same close reach on the port tack that they had maintained since before the dawn. They watched as Madden took his sun sight and went below to make his calculations and enter the position on the chart.

He came out on deck again and, turning to Perkinson, spoke for everyone to hear.

"I think it's time to pass the word to all hands," he said. "Don't you?"

Perkinson nodded agreement.

"Go ahead," he said. He lounged back upon his elbows and looked across the cockpit at the sea.

It was apparent that Madden was a veteran of many a planning conference. All that he said seemed to make the greatest of good sense. He created in the cockpit of that sailboat the atmosphere of a meeting room where note pads, ashtrays, yellow pencils with sharp points, and spaced water carafes were all at hand.

He skated past all but the practicalities that concerned them.

It was possible, he told them, that the three of them would be leaving *Avatar* Sunday night at 2230 just off the coast of the island that they would reach at that time.

They would be ashore for four or five hours, during which period *Avatar* would sail offshore to a calculated distance and return for them.

Then they would continue their race to the finish and do what they could to make up the lost time.

Lovell watched them from the wheel, Colleran up on the windward rail, Iacovino was farther forward, a beer in hand. Max was in the cockpit near the instrument bulkhead working on the chart that he was keeping of their position relative to the other racing boats that had reported themselves that morning.

"Why?" he said, raising his head suddenly. "Why are you going ashore there?"

"Because we have an assignment to go ashore," Bailey told him over his shoulder.

"From who?"

"That doesn't concern you."

"Hell it doesn't!" Colleran said.

"Look," Madden told him, "that's beside the point. If I thought you should know, I'd tell you. We have this assignment. If and when we are given the go, we go. Period."

"Did you know about this, John?" Colleran asked suddenly.

Lovell nodded.

"When?"

"Last August."

"Do you know what they are going to do?"

Lovell nodded.

"Then tell us. If we're a party to it, we ought to know."

"We are going to put a radio station off the air for a couple of days," Perkinson said. "The one that you hear all over the dial. It'd be no great loss if it were wiped off permanently, but we're just going to quiet it."

"Who the fuck cares if it goes on forever?" Iacovino asked. "Who has to listen?"

Lovell smiled.

"I do," Madden said. "I don't care generally, but specifically. It's an assignment for me. All these distractions are unnecessary. There's nothing to discuss. Lovell agreed—he's here and so are you on a paid vacation. You have no responsibility in the matter, and you aren't going to win anyhow. Are you?"

"How do you know that?" Max asked. "You're no expert. You don't have any idea of what our position is to the other boats in the class."

"You're right there," Madden said.

"Also," Max added, "I don't know how you're plotting our position, but you aren't doing it with that sextant."

"Right again," Madden told him. "But there isn't a navigator in this whole fleet who has a better reckoning.

"I get it four times a day. I could have it forty times if I wanted it. From the number two receiver."

He jerked his thumb at the cabin.

"Great," Max said, looking at Lovell. "The whole thing is a fake."

Lovell nodded, and moved the wheel to correct.

"That is piss poor," Max said bitterly.

"Isn't it, Frank?"

"You owed us our choice, John," Colleran said.

"You had a choice," Lovell told him. "You could have stayed home."

Colleran turned away angrily.

"That's completely phony, John," Max said quickly. "You knew we'd have hung ourselves to come. We put in ten years on this bomb. You don't just do that to go sailing. You do it because you're friends."

"Hey, Bailey, why don't you just pay us for the voyage?" Iacovino said. "Wouldn't have to listen to this bullshit.

"What the fuck do you care what they do, Maxie baby? They're the ones taking the risks."

"You stupid son of a bitch," Max told him. "Do you think I'm afraid?"

"I don't think anything. Sail the boat, will you?" he said to Lovell.

"The jib is soft, either harden up or change course. Something."

"What I can't reconcile, John," Colleran said, "is you played us like a couple of fish. Okay, Iacovino will go anywhere he has a berth so he can come down and screw himself into limbo, but you owed us more."

"I'm paying it," Lovell said simply. "I'm a bastard. Tell me something I don't know.

"I'd like to explain it better, but I can't. It seemed to me to be a small price to pay for a lot of gratification. I have the most to gain, I grant you that. But nobody is taking any great advantage of you. I'm taking the responsibility for the whole affair. I thought the pleasure would outweigh any other feelings. I still think so.

"Just what the hell are you doing that is so God-awful?"

"That's just it," Colleran said grimly. "I don't know."

"Frank," Perkinson said quietly, "do we look like a bunch of murderers or criminals? We're not laying waste to a territory. It's a very simple thing for all concerned."

"Are you going ashore with weapons?" Colleran asked directly.

"A grease gun, .45 caliber, a Mauser carbine, and a Springfield. But they won't be used except as a last resort."

"And a little dynamite or TNT."

"A little," Perkinson admitted.

"What else?"

"Six grenades, incendiary, and six antipersonnel. Some caps and fuses," Madden told him. "Does that sound like we're starting a war?"

"I'll tell you this, all of you," Colleran said. "If you had offered a hint of this operation to me on shore I never would have come. I owe you nothing in the way of help or loyalty on those grounds alone."

"What about your country?" Madden said. "What do you owe it? Nothing?"

Colleran's face flushed with anger.

"I'll tell you one thing—nobody as shallow as you should waste time trying to politicize. Not with me, anyway. I think you're sick.

"You present us with a *fait accompli* and then you offer your own delusions as a reason to close ranks and support you, as Americans. I hope your operation is better than your argument."

Madden looked at Perkinson and Amat, lips drawn in a thin sour line.

"Far as I'm concerned," he said, "the meeting is over. I know what I'm going to do, and you know what we have to do. If you want to keep up the discussion, go ahead. But be sure they understand that no one is to interfere with me."

He went below. Iacovino followed.

"Lunch menu for today," he bellowed, "tuna fish or ham and cheese. State your preference."

"Pass me," Max said glumly, and "forget Frank too."

"You're constipated," Iacovino said, "that's your trouble. Take some prune juice and clean out your pipes."

Max went up forward to sit with Colleran. They spoke at length. On the breeze, snatches of their conversation came to the three in the cockpit.

"Whole goddamn affair"; "simple-minded"; "knew they couldn't trust us until we're four hundred miles out"; "devious"; "demeaning."

Obviously it was small satisfaction. The expletives became more frequent and more violent.

Of the two, Colleran was the most intransigent. His anger turned to an icy, controlled antipathy.

Lovell analyzed it objectively. He had expected a different attitude—shared cynicism and agreement, even admiration for a good trade—a new boat for four hours of co-operation.

Surely they weren't so much different from him.

"You should have brought two more Iacovinos," Perkinson remarked. "If I thought these two were so much more moral than you, I'd never have agreed to the crew."

"They surprise me too," Lovell told him. "I should choose my friends more carefully."

Iacovino handed up a large plate of sandwiches and a supply of drinks, and followed them out on deck. Lovell took one and eyed it distastefully: tuna fish with a slather of mayonnaise. The two pieces of bread should not have been so mismated. Oil from the tuna had soaked into the bottom slice.

He bit into it and it began to dissolve in his hands.

"Pretty crappy sandwich man, ain't I?" Iacovino said. "Could be worse—if it was dinner."

"I want to change the watches," Colleran said, coming down from his forward position. "Put Max and me together from now on. No need to keep up the pretext any longer. We are going to be handling the boat, so we might as well work the same watch the rest of the way."

"Make your decision?" Perkinson said idly.

Colleran looked at him calmly.

"Is there a choice?" he asked.

Perkinson shook his head.

"No more will a sack of our rice, a barrel of our oil or a gram of our minerals be taken away. Our land and its unlimited resources and riches will now improve our own lives. It is not for the gorging of parasites."

BOCA GRANDE 3 / 10

They passed the remaining hours of Saturday as formally as possible on a boat the size of theirs. Only Iacovino paid any attention to the race. At intervals, if he spotted a sail, he would pick up the binoculars to see if he could identify it.

When Colleran and Max went off watch they removed themselves to the forecabin. On deck they were quiet and withdrawn, refusing any conversational gambit, and speaking only when necessary.

Their log entries were as stiff as those on a naval vessel. There were no more of the rhapsodic comments that they had entered along the way as the spirit had moved them.

In the main cabin, adjacent to the navigator's space, Madden and Amat now worked openly at their preparations for the assault on Boca Grande.

Under Perkinson's eye, they went over a file of aerial photographs of the installations, photographs so detailed that even filled garbage and latrine pits could be seen.

There were other pictures taken at ground level of the power supply that kept Boca Grande on the air, of the bases of the two three-hundred-foot steel towers that supported its antenna, and of the fittings that connected the support cables to the poured concrete anchors.

There was a strip map inked with the route from the beach to the escarpment above, to where Boca Grande had been sited.

They spent an hour over them, refreshing and restating what they had committed to memory weeks before.

Then they began on the equipment.

There was a flat steel box lined with styrofoam molded to carry six mercury fulminate detonators—pencil-shaped copper cylinders with hollow ends into which fuse could be fitted and crimped.

Madden went over the ammunition clips for the grease gun. He wiped each round clean and replaced them exactly, the pin end of each set firmly against the rear of the clip.

He took up the carbine and finally the Springfield. He examined bolts, extractors, ejectors, and, lastly, the single rounds for their clips with more interest than simply a workman's care for a tool.

He looked over the grenades for a sign of rust and for dents in the incendiaries.

After each item had passed his scrutiny, he turned it over to Amat, who inspected it as well. Then Amat sealed them into a waterproof case and stowed them below the navigator's bunk.

Perkinson lounged opposite and watched.

"Pretty basic, isn't it?" Lovell said, taking a cup of coffee.

"Pretty basic," Perkinson agreed. "Operation Simple-minded."

Madden glanced up at him sourly.

"Bailey thinks it's beneath his capabilities," Perkinson said. "And he's probably right. He needs something grander."

He smiled at Lovell.

Madden glanced at his watch, flipped on the power switches of the receiver-transmitter unit above the chart space, and plugged a set of headphones into the jack.

He tuned and listened, checking the time on his watch with *Avatar*'s chronometer. Then he tapped a signal into the continuous wave with the radio telegrapher's bug at his hand, made a note on his message pad, and cut the switches. The routine took less than two minutes.

"Still no go," he told Perkinson quietly. "All we have to show for this eight months is a sunburn and bills."

"Thus it goes," Perkinson said. "You'll get your chance."

Madden grunted and spun the dials on the standard receiver. Boca Grande came in loud and clear, filling the cabin with imprecation so painfully enunciated that one could hear the announcer's aspiration.

"Sick son of a bitch," Madden said. He translated: "Their hands still dripping blood from their organized thuggery and dismemberment of the People's Republic . . .

"Shit," he said. "That isn't even a country. People locked into an economy that can't provide for half of them tell the world how to live. Look at the contributions to the betterment of man. The banana, the pineapple, and the sugar stalk."

"You're getting passionate, Bailey," Amat said.

"That's what comes from the half-assed idealists. By the time they finish talking, there's a power vacuum that's filled with a mouth instead of a nation with a conscience and a sense of responsibility. Am I wrong?"

They had sailed all day in a steadily increasing breeze that built from fifteen to over twenty knots. Now they began to make their way far enough to the west so that the spinnaker was called for.

They hoisted the sail, the rounded shoulders of the spinnaker curving out ahead of the bow as they trimmed sheet and guy to the best point.

The needle of the Kenyon inched ahead as *Avatar* rose upon the swell, the westering sun setting its colors agleam.

At 2200, they picked up the loom of the light at Punta Maisi. Now it was time to change course again to hug that dark, unfriendly coast until they reached the drop point.

Again it was Colleran's trick on the wheel. He had just come on. He steered with precision and daring, taking the seas with accommodation, easing and firming *Avatar* along with less and less interval between rushing crest and slowing trough.

There was no moon, but the sky was brilliant with stars and, staring up at the masthead and beyond, Lovell fancied he could see the constellations moving at dizzying speed to the northern heavens.

"Come to two four zero," Madden said. "Two four zero."

Colleran didn't reply. Instead, he spoke to Lovell.

"Give us another ten minutes of this, will you, John?" he asked.

"We'll hold for a few minutes longer," Lovell said.

"Do what he tells you to!" Perkinson snapped from his station just forward of the mast. "The debate's over."

Madden came purposefully out of the companionway and moved to the wheel.

"Get off," he said to Colleran, and closed his hands upon the wheel.

There was a momentary struggle between them. In that small interval the bow of the boat fell off the course and suddenly overcorrected, came back too far.

The great sail went immediately overtight across its whole expanse, as suddenly loosened as the bow came across the wind, lost drive, and snapped sharply full again, driving against sheet, guy, and mast fitting.

Amat lost his concentration at the movement behind him and eight feet of his line ran out before he could snub it.

Once more the sail snapped full. Max tried to take up the slack with his foreguy, then lost control of his line as well. The spinnaker pole slammed forward to the headstay, missing Iacovino by inches, the pole twisted up and bowed.

Lovell seized the line from Max's winch and threw his weight upon it.

"Winch it!" he shouted, and to the two at the wheel—"Bear off, head off, goddamn it!"

Slowly, agonizingly slowly, *Avatar* turned with a wrench in the sea, the rudder hard over, and the next wave broke just under her stern and flung her hard off the wind. The spinnaker, empty at the top and winched tight across the whole width of the foot, now filled again, snapping upward and outward with a crack like a tree splitting.

Aware only of that ominous sound, Lovell neither heard nor saw the bell-fitting on the mast fracture.

He did see the inboard end of the pole spring free and deal Perkinson a stunning blow on the side of the head that dropped him in a heap half through the open forehatch. Then the pole flew forward like a monstrous steel-shod arrow.

Before they could get to Perkinson, they brought the spinnaker down, the mass of tangled line and bright-colored nylon heaped in the dim light of the stars.

Then Lovell and Madden went forward and eased him down through the forehatch while Colleran held the boat as steadily as he could in the eye of the wind.

There was a trickle of blood from nose and ear that was already coagulating. His right eye was open and stared at them, unblinking, as they slid him into the port berth.

"Hold him there," Lovell said, gasping for breath. His arms and shoulders were suddenly without strength and his knees were jelly.

He leaned against a hanging locker for minutes, it seemed.

Amat's face appeared in the hatchway at deck level.

"Is he all right?"

"Don't know," Lovell mumbled, and then more loudly and plainly, "I don't know!"

Max's face appeared too, and Iacovino's. He motioned them back.

"Clean up the deck," he said. "Come to a course. It's better for him than this."

"What about the engine?" Max said. "Should we turn on the engine?"

"Clean up!" Lovell shouted again. "Clean up and come to two four zero. You can do that, can't you?"

There was an immediate rush of feet overhead, as though they were eager to be occupied.

"All right," Lovell said. "You better get on that radio of yours and get hold of a doctor."

"He's just knocked out," Madden said. "His color's coming back and he's stirring."

"He's rolling," Lovell said, "not stirring. It's the hull that's moving him. Get the radio going. Do you know the band?"

Madden nodded and moved to the aft cabin.

Staring down at Perkinson, Lovell heard his movements at the transmitter but he didn't hear him speak.

Lovell took a handkerchief that had served as both napkin and sweatband and gently wiped away the blood that had thickened around Perkinson's right nostril, down the gray-stubbled chin and the corner of his mouth. Straightening, he called out impatiently:

"What's the matter?"

There was no answer.

Swearing, he moved back into the main cabin. Madden stood halfway up the three steps that led to the deck, a transistor board in his hand.

"What's wrong, I asked you?" he said, and knew the answer.

Madden spoke calmly but his face was pale and he licked his lips over his little speech.

"There won't be any transmission," he said, "until tomorrow night. Maybe not then. And don't try anything or I'll toss it over the side."

Lovell looked at him, measuring the distance, and remembered Perkinson's warning. He shrugged.

"Okay," he said. "He would have handled it differently if it had been you."

"It's my decision," Madden said. "I made it. Maybe he would have made a different one. He's fifty-five. I'm not."

Above them, in the cockpit, listening, Lovell could see the others. There was a stealthy movement from Max.

"Don't," Madden said quietly.

"Maybe I can help him," Max said roughly. "That's all I want to do. Is he conscious?"

"You know," Colleran said calmly from the helm, "it can't hurt to ask for a doctor in the fleet. We can just report the symptoms to him. How can that interfere?"

"Can't be done," Madden said icily. "You stay out of it. If it hadn't been for you, the whole thing would never have happened."

There was a hiss behind Lovell and, thinking it was Perkinson, he moved into the tiny forecabin again. It was Iacovino, his massive head hanging down through the hatch.

"Say the word," he mouthed, "and I'll bust his fucking head for him with the winch handle."

"Can't," Lovell said. "Not now."

Max pushed into the forecastle. He shook his head.

"Christ," he said. "He looks like he's had a stroke. Did you take a pulse?"

Lovell shook his head.

"Talk to him," Max said, "stop acting like he's not here."

He himself began immediately to speak, calmly and lightly, though he swallowed often and his own neck and face were flushed.

He turned Perkinson's head to the right and bent low over him.

Behind his ear there was a half-round impression that seemed, when the dim light of the cabin played upon it, to be as much an outward curve.

Then he took his pulse and listened with his ear low to Perkinson's chest for his heartbeat.

"Strong enough. Real strong," he said. "Come on, Perk, you can hear me, can't you? Talk to me a minute. Come out of that."

Amat appeared at his elbow with the big first-aid kit and opened it on the other bunk.

"Spirits of ammonia," he offered, but Max shook his head.

"Might be too strong," he said. "Wait a few minutes. Come on, now, get back here. Back."

Perkinson's lips moved stiffly, as though swollen.

Then there was speech from Perkinson, impatient speech, as though a whole sea of words were waiting to be spoken. His right eye opened and the left too, but round and staring and off center, the pupil moving unwilled from the outer eye corner to the nose.

Max reached under Perkinson's T-shirt and rubbed his chest firmly and his stomach.

"What are you doing that for?" Amat said.

"I don't know," Max told him. "I saw a nurse doing it to my wife after she had a baby. Maybe it helps the breathing."

"No baby," Perkinson said suddenly and clearly. "No son. Stops right here!"

"Back," he said, and was silent again.

"We're going to move you, Perk," Max told him. "Going to give you the good bunk in the main cabin, where we can keep an eye on you. Come on," he told Lovell. "Take his feet. Amat, you watch his head—support it under his neck. We can't keep him in here."

He was heavier than he seemed. Caring for his condition made it the more difficult to ease him through the narrow bulkhead between fore and main cabin.

There was a suppressed curse from Lovell. Perkinson had lost control of bowels and bladder and it was Lovell who knew it first.

Now it was necessary to clean out the leeward bunk in the main cabin, to take down the dining table, and to clean away the remains of dinner and the clothes, books, and tools that had come to rest there.

Madden was braced against the navigator's table. He had removed the grease gun from its plastic case and had it ready to hand, the ejector cover up, the weapon cocked.

Seeing this, the three of them paused in mid-journey.

Amat shook his head sadly.

"Put it away," he said, "you don't need that."

"If the rest of them tell me that, I will," Madden said quietly. "You and I are on the same side."

Impressed with his own solicitude, accepting the foulness on his hands, and the offense to his nose, Lovell was not angered but pained by him.

He straightened up, his back muscles aching from the short, unbalanced carry, and spoke quietly.

"I want you off this boat as much as you want to get off. More. So unload that thing and put it away before you kill some other poor bastard."

Madden accepted it with a nod, drew the clip from the weapon, and unloaded it. Then he unscrewed the pipe barrel and dropped it in his pocket.

"That's all I wanted to hear," he said.

It was midnight before they managed to make Perkinson

comfortable, assembling bedding out of spare toweling, contriving a kind of diaper after they washed him painstakingly with warm fresh water and mild soap and dried him. As they finished, he vomited quietly on his pillow. Amat and Max watched and waited until they thought it was over. It was not. They washed him again, and kept a kettle warm on the stove against the next requirement.

Then they had to rinse out the soiled bedding in the tiny sink in the head and fasten clothing and towels haphazardly to the lifelines and stanchions, although it could not dry before the morning.

They opened all the ventilators and the ports and sprayed a full can of deodorizer from forepeak to engine compartment. The stench not only remained, but combined with stale tobacco smoke, dregs in beer cans and wine bottles, clothing worn overlong, diesel oil exhalations, deck shoes, and milk spills into an essence. This not only overwhelmed their noses but brought tears to the eyes. Flooding up from the cabin at the hatch, it made the helmsman's station almost untenable. Whoever was at the wheel crouched on the windward rail, head high and cocked away.

Lovell withdrew to the deck last. He took a bottle of rum up with him and they clustered on deck, passing the bottle from hand to hand through the hours, sipping it slowly and passing it before it was requested.

Overhead the stars were firm in their courses. Just beyond reach through the lifelines, a wave from the east curled and coalesced in white and dark foam. All was unchanged; all but the pleasures and the anticipations, the risks and the responsibilities—these were now in shards and shreds.

Iacovino took over the wheel from Colleran and chain-smoked borrowed cigarettes with his nose pointed to the breeze. At intervals Amat or Max went below to see to the patient.

Through this night they heard his voice, clearly sometimes, his diction as sharp as though he were coming on watch and speaking companionably to a mate below. Then he would tremble and fail and syllables would run one upon the other as though a radio tuner had halted in mid-turn between three stations. Unwillingly, they set their minds to disentangle this assemblage of croak and suspiration and labial. It was as though they could keep him among them, whole again, if they did so.

Until the false dawn failed and the sun rose they listened wearily yet untired. Perkinson gave back from his bruised brain whatever lay there: passion and pleasure, obscurity and vividness, and, remarkably, like a shaft of light, mention of themselves.

There was more. Grocery lists. Remembered errands. Aphorisms, book titles, street names, women.

It was no privilege to hear it. It exacerbated more than screams. It admitted them to a secret place. They longed not to be there.

After one prolonged enunciation that ended in a choking, stertorous, rasping rattle, Iacovino suggested a shot of morphine.

"For Christ's sake, give him a needle," he demanded. "You've got it, give it to him. What are you saving it for?"

In the morning he lost strength. The periods of speech became less frequent. Finally he was silent.

Amat and Max strapped him loosely into his bunk and damped his lips with brandy and water at intervals, and left him.

By midmorning the blazing sun drained the remaining strength from them.

Seeing it, Lovell turned them all off watch, set the sails himself, and took the wheel, alone in the cockpit.

For twenty minutes he sat there fighting sleep, hearing fitful snores from cabin and foredeck. Then Madden came up.

He seemed to have aged over the night. His eyes were red. Small pouches appeared beneath them where only yesterday the skin of his face was taut and unwrinkled. His chin and cheeks were stubbled. There were some gray bristles there.

He dipped a bucket of seawater and sluiced it over himself, and then another. Splashing Lovell in the process, he muttered an apology.

It mattered little to him. An ice bath or an hour in a sauna would have had no effect.

Madden cleared his throat.

"Makes it very difficult," he said, "for Amat and me. I mean to go ashore."

"I imagine so," Lovell said.

"We'll go," Madden said, "but it won't be easy."

"I guess not."

"We'll miss him," Madden said, picking at his thumbnail. "I mean his experience. Of course, Mat has plenty. I think the two of us can still handle it."

Lovell grunted noncommittally, refusing to ease the way.

"I wonder," Madden said, staring to sea, "if one of the crew would go. If it would be a good idea to try and take another man along."

"Try," Lovell said dryly.

"You make any suggestions?" Madden said, his face stonily without expression.

"No."

"I didn't think so. I didn't think you would."

Lovell looked at him angrily.

"If you want help, goddamn it, ask for it, plead for it! We all do it, you know. We don't put our lives together like a stone fort. What makes you think you're any different?

"Your plans and your receiver that gives you your position ten times a day and your old weapons with the new barrels?

"You're just a plain ordinary fellow like the rest of us, sometimes you're more screwed up than other times. And here you are with one of the other times."

He leaned toward him over the wheel.

"You can still handle it, can you? Then handle it!"

Madden stared back at him fixedly, as though to peer inside the dark lenses of Lovell's sunglasses, to search out what lay there.

He licked his lips where the saltwater from the bucket had dried around his mouth. The movement was so ingenuous that it inspired sympathy.

"Here," Lovell said. He tossed him a tube of lip balm. "Smear it on before they crack wide open."

Madden looked at the tube moodily.

"I'll handle it," he said. "I'm not one of the brilliant ones. I can't find the answers fast, but I find them. I'll get through it. I got through last night, lying there right next to him. After a couple of hours of it I didn't even think about him. I just chalked him off the organizational chart."

He wiped his lips with the lip balm, methodically.

"What about that?"

Lovell shrugged.

"He's not your father. Just a fellow employee."

"He's not an easy man to work with. You can't impress him. He gives you the feeling that you're not adequate in an area you don't know about. Never gets angry, just that endless toleration. It's tough to live with. He made his point. He shook my confidence, but I'll get it back."

"Sure," Lovell said. "That's all you need, confidence. And stop talking about him in the present.

"Tell me," he said, "who were you thinking of asking to come ashore with you?"

"Iacovino."

Lovell laughed.

"He wouldn't go ashore if you had his favorite movie star waiting for him on the beach with her legs apart. And he couldn't get up to the top, and he'd sound like a moose when you get into that cane field.

"You weren't thinking of Iacovino. You were thinking of me. What put it in your head—what Perk said about me?"

"Probably."

"I'm going with you, Bailey," Lovell said. "If you get the word today, and I'm sure you will, I'm going to go. It's better to go than to sit on board waiting for you. But don't be sanguine about it. There are things that I know I can't do any more."

"What?"

"I won't tell you," he said. "You'll be more alert that way."

"While their situation is well-known to be a disaster, Our Leader reported that we have the lowest cost of living in the world. Our inflation rate has sunk from eighty per cent to zero. Our cost of living rose by only two point five per cent and our wages have risen by twenty-one per cent. Can anyone doubt the success of our economy?"

BOCA GRANDE 3 / 11

After lunch, a meal of warm beans and cool luncheon meat that appealed to no one, Lovell turned *Avatar* over to Colleran with only a mention of the course, and went below with Amat and Madden to be briefed.

What he remembered from the past was not a comprehensive recollection of any single operation, but only a scatter of scenes and impressions.

When they went over their plan it was as though he had never been away; he was swallowed up in the problem and their solution.

A number of diversions were under way already. A drop in the mountains miles to the west. A simulated raid had occurred the night before on the northern coast. A series of airspace incursions was scheduled to begin at dusk over the westernmost harbor town.

Practice naval exercises were to take place east of the Windward Passage, whether the attack on Boca Grande was mounted or not.

Madden tuned Boca Grande in at low volume as they spoke, and Mat translated as the announcer reported activity. He was succeeded by an Olympian voice reporting the number of casualties and the units involved.

". . . the engagement lasted four hours before the surviving attackers withdrew before our outnumbered but undaunted defenders. The following losses were inflicted: sunk—four motor torpedo boats, two high-speed personnel landing craft. Damaged by our gunfire after removal of crews and invading parties —two personnel landing craft. Damaged in hull, but escaped pursuit—two motor torpedo boats, one corvette armed with support-type missiles. Our losses—minimal damage to one motor torpedo boat."

"A quiet night on the Coral Sea," Mat said.

They turned to the strip maps that plotted the route up the four-hundred-foot height to Boca Grande's level.

They showed Lovell photo sequences of the landing and the simplified engineering drawings that indicated the placement of the charges that would weaken or snap the antenna mast cables. The charges and the prevailing winds would bring the structure down.

Watching and listening, Lovell imagined the man hours of discussion and consideration of this problem. The expertise distilled from so many varying disciplines.

Behind him, Perkinson stirred in the bunk. A froth bubbled from his lips.

The intensity of the odor in the cabin was less strong or their own sensitivity to it had declined.

Perkinson was only a factor now. They made adjustment

for him. He interrupted their sleep, made their meals impossible, upset their plans, and offended their noses. But they went on. There would be an end to it. They would have their accomplishment, they would give him care and attention soon. Sometime soon.

It was not their fault that he had crossed the line between man and burden.

Max came below, and Madden took him through the operation of the special transmitter. He gave him the recognition signal that had to be fed into it with the key, and showed him the drop area on a 1:10,000 chart.

They were to go ashore at 2100 hours. *Avatar* would sail a course reciprocal to the approach for two and a half hours, and then return to the drop-off point in as close to five hours of total time as could be managed.

There was an additional half-hour allowance for the pickup.

"Then what?" Colleran asked from the wheel.

"Finish the race," Madden told him. "When you're forty miles offshore, get on the radio and ask for assistance for Perk."

"That will be forty-eight hours without treatment."

"Acceptable," Madden said.

"By whom?" Colleran demanded.

"Everyone," Madden said, "including him. He would want it that way."

Colleran sniffed and shook his head.

"Written down somewhere on him. 'What to do in case of injury—continue as planned.'"

Madden ignored the comment. He turned wearily to Lovell.

"I've got to get some sleep. Will you wake me at fifteen thirty?"

Lovell nodded. Madden slid into his navigator's bunk. Drawing the blanket up over his head, he seemed immediately to be asleep.

"You know," Colleran said, "I'm goddamn tired, and so are Max and Charlie."

Lovell nodded. Colleran's eyes were red-rimmed, irritated by the salt from the spray. He had done more than his share of time on the helm since Perkinson's injury, and it showed. There was salt caked in every fold of skin, the chafing in crotch and armpit that could become saltwater sores, boils, carbuncles.

"It won't be much longer," he said, placating, "twenty-four hours at most."

"It won't end there," Colleran said. "What about if you don't get back? Suppose you get your asses shot off? Suppose they intercept us? Suppose we have to get back ourselves?"

"Which do you want to talk about? Pick one."

"If you don't get back?"

"Get to port as fast as you can—engine, sail, or both."

"And what do I say? You're owner and captain."

"Madden will give you a number to call when you get in. It'll all be taken care of.

"Don't say anything. Say you lost us over the side in the same jibe that busted Perkinson's head."

"Except that it's never happened in an ocean race since 1933."

"That was that father and two sons," Max said. "But that was transatlantic."

"Tell them I was your father," Lovell suggested. "Tell anything you want to tell anybody. You're not teaching history now, you're a part of it. Realpolitik."

"I've been part of it before. On principle then."

Lovell shook his head.

"Come on, Frank," he said tiredly, "bug off. You were caught up in a cataclysm. You acted on pieces of paper, draft notices, orders to report, illustrations of Washington at Valley Forge, the Gettysburg Address. You didn't make any assessments.

"I like you. You're my friend. You do have more principle than most—than I, than Perkinson. Well and good—if you hadn't sensed an appreciation of that in me, then you'd not have been my friend either. Or Max's, I suppose.

"Politics erodes principle. What it comes down to is for you to evaluate what's between you and me. After we get off there's nothing to prevent you from skating off for Jamaica, is there?

"Well, is there?"

Colleran shook his head.

"I wouldn't do that. You know I wouldn't," he said flatly.

"That's the point. You're using us. Goddamn it, I'm a man, not a puppet for you and for such reasons—you're corrupt, John, and I hope you realize how corrupt."

"That's for me to live with," Lovell told him. "You're way off course."

Lovell took the wheel. When Colleran rose to give way, a paperback book fell from his hip pocket—one of the ten volumes he had brought with him in his duffel. Lovell picked it up and handed it to him. George Sorel, *Reflections on Violence.*

Colleran took it and flung it over the side.

Madden shouted at him from below in a rage.

"Cut that, goddamn it! All of you. Nothing goes over the side until tomorrow—not even a cigarette butt!"

Lovell raised his eyebrows.

"Operational discipline," he said. "That's what we're under now.

"Seal the head," he bellowed, laughing. "No more shit in the sea! You men have been chosen for your mental and your physical strength! You're an elite! Act like it!"

The shouting roused the others. Iacovino came out and dropped to the deck forward, dejected, dispirited. From habit he squinted up at the set of the genoa—the one that they had set after Perkinson's injury. It was as heavy as carved wood and did little in this middling breeze to improve speed or trim.

"For Christ's sake," he said, "change the sail! At least give the impression that we're racing. Come on, goddamn it."

He stood up and pounded with his foot on the hatch cover.

"Right on, Foredeck, or Foreskin, or whatever your name is," Lovell shouted.

"All hands to change head sails! Come on, everybody up!"

It took them almost ten minutes, moving like automatons, to change the sail, to Lovell's running commentary.

At 1615 hours on *Avatar*'s chronometer, Madden came on deck.

"We're going," he said quietly.

"Did you report the damage to Perkinson?" Lovell asked.

He shook his head.

"I can't. The transmission is limited. Continuous wave, not voice."

"Just a signal."

"That's right."

"Must make you feel like a white rat. Get a beep and you're off."

"Where do we launch?"

"Midships. Right there," Lovell told him, "where the lifeline can be opened. But you don't want to bring up the gear yet, do you?"

Madden rubbed the back of his hand across his eyes.

"No, of course not. But I want to be ready."

Lovell looked at him more closely and recognized the appearance of that weight that lies upon those who plan and construct or decide at the time when the first step toward realization is taken.

It is commitment and it becomes a definite poundage that loads the area between the shoulders like a back pack.

This burden is so real that the thumbs reach to ease the imaginary pack straps or a hand may wander to the small of the back to adjust the mass for easier carry. The fingers are stretched and the shoulders shaken as though to assure the animal that the load lies simply upon the mind.

These movements and motions are rarely seen. Usually they are hidden by reserve, taciturnity, or disguised behind a flood of conversation, mordant humor.

Having no gift for wry comment or self-mockery, Madden was now behaving like a newly appointed commander committing his troops to battle for the first time.

In less than an hour he drew up four or five operational checklists and compared them with all the drafts he had prepared to this point. He changed the order of equipping the landing dinghy and changed it back, and finally he rigged a clipboard at the deck stanchion that Lovell had pointed out to him and attached a pen to it so that he could have one final review of all details before they left *Avatar*.

Then he went below and laid out upon his navigator's bunk and chart table the equipment that they would take ashore with them, the weapons in their plastic envelopes, the three small back packs. It was not an overwhelming amount of materiel.

From behind, he heard his name spoken softly, almost as though it were a whisper inside his own head. A persistent whisper.

"Bailey," Perkinson said, and a bit louder, "Bailey."

Madden turned to him where he lay upon the bunk, the board up along its length to keep him from sliding out, the fingers of his left hand playing upon the thin nylon line that Amat and Max had contrived to keep him from rolling about.

"You're ready, Bailey?" he said clearly.

"I'm ready," Madden said.

"That's fine," Perkinson said, "fine. I knew you would be. You're dependable. I'm sorry I'm not going to go. You understand why I'm not going, Bailey, don't you?"

Madden nodded.

"Of course," he said. "Do you have any pain?"

Perkinson waved his hand almost briskly.

"Nothing. No pain. I'll be fine. I'm sorry that I can't go. If we could wait a day or two I could go. Do what I'm supposed to do. Backstop you. Not necessary. You know that. Right?"

"Right," Bailey said. "How about a drink of water? Or tea? I'll get Berliner."

"No tea. Listen to me. It is very important that you perform and get back. Hear? Not only to you, but to me. Right? You have to go"—he touched his stomach with his forefinger as he spoke—"you have to perform, and you have to come back. Know why?"

"Why?" Madden mumbled. "Look, you have to stop talking. You're just tiring yourself."

Perkinson frowned and the tightening of his face muscles seemed to pain him.

"You're my contribution to the future, Bailey, that's why. That's what I have done. That's more important than king and country. Don't forget it."

He rose upon his elbow agitatedly.

"Don't forget it!" He fell back upon the bunk exhausted.

Max dropped lightly down from above and interposed himself between them.

"Good boy, Perk," he said, "good boy. If you can talk that well, you're improving. Let's try the tea again. We'll put some rum in it. Warm tea with rum."

Perkinson smiled a twisted smile at him.

"One favor," he said. "Stop calling me good boy. I'm a man. Grown. Up and over and down the other side."

His voice trailed off and when he spoke again there was a regression.

"Hay's mowed," he said, "stacked. Stored."

That evening, as though in compensation for the disquiet and discord, was the loveliest that they had encountered. Perhaps because they were approaching the land mass, the breeze, though mild, had a particular sweetness to it, an odor of green and blossom.

The sun glowed on the sea. Ahead of them it tinted the water with pure dark red and that melded to purple as *Avatar* came on in silence, west by north.

Dinner was over. Below, in the galley, Iacovino was stowing the pots and utensils. The muted clash of dishes and silver and his humming were an oddly domestic obbligato.

Lovell sat at the helm, composed, silent, *Avatar* almost sailing herself across the darkening, glassy surface.

Colleran sat with his back against the cabin bulkhead, as though deliberately ranging himself outside these influences. He stared over the stern.

"You have company," he said quietly, and pointed.

In another light they might never have been certain, but the rays of the lowering sun picked out in a violent pink two sails on the horizon miles astern of them.

Max put the binoculars on them.

"Can't tell," he said finally, "but they could be Class A. One of them is a big boat."

"Sure," Colleran said, scanning them himself. "They're following this breeze inshore. Must be dead out there."

Madden came out on deck dressed in a pair of green coveralls and sneakers.

"Great," he said bitterly. "The whole goddamn ocean to sail on and they have to follow us."

"Sound tactics," Max said. "Go where the breeze is. Keep the boat moving."

"Son of a bitch," Iacovino said. "Maybe we're first."

He grinned at Madden.

"Be funny if they followed us right up on the shore, wouldn't it? It'd look like D-day in 1776."

"How far away are they?" Madden asked.

Colleran shrugged.

"Max?"

"Four miles. Five."

Lovell looked at his watch.

"Relax," he said. "It'll be full dark in an hour. They won't see us after that—or we them. It could even help you, if we're part of a fleet.

"Be careful," he added to Colleran, "when you turn offshore again. Keep your eyes peeled."

At eight o'clock all but a sliver of the corona had disappeared magically into the western sea as though past an edge, and with it the boats astern.

The wind, having blown steadily all the day and evening, finally brought in a thin cover of cloud. The edge of that small front was marked by a breeze of just over ten miles an hour—enough to ruffle the surface of the sea and increase their speed somewhat. They moved according to Max's calculations and his transmissions to Madden's source, to a point ten miles offshore.

Now there was a stronger odor from the land mass. It was the only indication that it was there or existed at all. It was a presence felt, just there ahead, but nowhere up and down that coast could any of them see a single gleam of light.

They went on in almost absolute silence, the cabin lights, the port and starboard running lights, and the white light at the masthead dark.

There was only the weak sheen from the binnacle to be seen on board.

At 2100 hours Amat and Madden brought up the dinghy, a four-by-four-foot package all tucked in about itself. Colleran ordered the genoa sheets eased and *Avatar* ghosted on, almost upright.

Lovell posted himself at the rail, the weapons and the packs in a controllable heap between deckhouse and rail. He stayed there, peering ahead the while and fancying that he could hear surf breaking, raising his eyes from ocean surface to a height quite preposterous for any elevation in the hemisphere. Finally he lost all confidence in his ability to see or to hear anything and he became certain that they would momentarily run this boat and this crew far up on the beach just ahead, that *Avatar* would stand momentarily exactly upon her keel and then fall like a dead elephant upon her side. The side opposite him.

"Land," Iacovino said hoarsely.

Then it came clearer and closer, as though placed there just at the moment of sighting.

Iacovino let the lead line down from the bow without a splash. Behind him in the forehatch, Max waited.

"Six," he hissed. "Six."

Max closed the hatch silently, moments passed, and he raised the hatch again.

"Eight," Iacovino said. "Seven and a half, eight."

Once more Max disappeared—this time for a shorter interval—and he returned for yet another reading.

"Five five," Iacovino said.

"We're here," Max told them in the cockpit. "That's it. Right on the head. Matches the chart exactly."

Leaving the wheel, Colleran freed the genoa sheet himself, the sail flapping loud in the quiet, the sheet block rattling in the stillness as though rapped by a hand.

They came on, groping as though blindfolded, committed to the man on the bow and his lead weight and the varied rags that marked the depth beneath the hull.

As he read the markings, Iacovino communicated to them in the darkness some of his own trepidation.

"Five even," he said, and then in what seemed only seconds of time, "four, three-five, three, three scant."

Madden and Amat were beside Lovell now, staring ahead with him at the land ahead. Far to the east and well above the surface of the sea there was a dull glow of orange, and another, distant but apparent.

"Cane fire," Amat whispered.

"Two scant," Iacovino said.

Colleran spun the wheel, heading *Avatar* into the wind. The sails flapped sharply and then fell to a soft rustling as he held the boat bow on to the breeze.

Madden freed the dinghy lashing and pulled the $CO_2$ lanyards. It hissed to accommodating size. Lovell opened the pelican hook at the stanchion and the two eased it over the side and down upon the quiet sea.

Amat passed the equipment to Madden, and then a number of short lengths of line with which Madden lashed it in place. Then Lovell toed the boat in toward *Avatar*'s side and held it there.

"One moment," Amat whispered and disappeared into the cabin.

"What the Christ did he forget," Madden hissed angrily, "his totem?"

The dinghy drifted back to the limit of its painter and Lovell was aware of a hand upon his shoulder and the white blur of Colleran's face as he leaned through *Avatar*'s lifelines.

"We'll be back, John," he said. "Don't worry."

Amat dropped lightly down in the stern of the dinghy.

"I said good-bye to him. To Perk," he told them.

They unshipped the paddles, drifting back as *Avatar* went slowly about, feeling her wake beneath the rubber bottom of the dinghy.

They drew apart, hearing the click of the winch ratchets, seeing the jib and main fill and set to firmness in the breeze, and the dim curves of the transom and sheer as she moved away into the darkness and left them alone off the silent shore.

Amat checked his compass and pointed to the course and

they went in, Lovell and Madden dipping the short paddles in silent unison, Amat steering with the compass set upon a pack between his knees. Lovell's mouth was dry. There was a lump of fear or exertion in his chest.

In ten minutes they saw a curl of white foam on a wave ahead. There was a surf, but a low one, that promised an easy landing.

They paused to check their reference again, broadside to the shore. Then they squared the stern of the dinghy to the surf and dug their paddles in once, twice, three times. But they were lifted too soon, and could not maintain themselves behind the crest, but moved ahead of it. The forward section of the dinghy fell away and into the trough ahead, filled and stopped, and in seconds they pitchpoled and floundered in the warm sea.

Lovell glimpsed Amat, struggling in the water with a musclebound thrashing stroke, his eyes rolling widely.

He caught the collar of his coverall and together they made their way to where Madden was attempting to hold back the overturned dinghy. Seizing the line that circled it at the gunwales, they managed to right it and floated it through the curling, creaming surf into the shallows off the beach.

Now straining at the pull of the sea, they waded ashore and dragged themselves unsteadily above the wave line, lifted up dinghy and burden, and made for the darkness before them, away from the pale cold sand strip to the cover of rising ground.

They walked as though drunk, without co-ordination, one of them now thrusting ahead, another back upon his heels, unconsciously adjusting their movements on shore to the hours on board *Avatar*, the burden that they bore like an oddly shaped treasure that each was attempting to pull away from his companions.

In common agreement they lowered it to the sand and knelt to draw breath. Then they raised it again, and this time, with deliberate steps and putting their feet down as widely as possible, they came into deep coarse grass that was sectored off by the wind and waves along the shore into what seemed like paths. Finally they were in thickening undergrowth where, with some screen around them, they halted again and deflated the dinghy, unloaded it, rolled it into the tight parcel it had been, and slung weapons and packs for the climb.

They moved off toward the escarpment ahead, Amat in the lead, moving easily for three or four hundred yards. The ground had been represented with exactness on the maps and photographs they had studied.

Then Amat halted suddenly, the barrel of the submachine gun raised, and he could be seen peering ahead.

"Logs," he whispered finally. "Trees down."

Madden gestured violently.

"So what? Go ahead!"

"All the way across—look." He waved the unencumbered arm.

Dim as the light was, they could see stark and sharply limned against the sky a mass of limbs, great lengths of log, some of them eight feet through, leaning at angles, propped and heaped, one upon another, some with their massive crowns still leafed and rustling in the night breeze.

"Go on up," Madden said abruptly. "Find a way up. We're behind schedule already.

"The bastards," he added bitterly. "They did this in the last two months. They've cut off our whole ravine."

"Terrible waste of wood. Tragic," Mat muttered. "And cut off our whole ravine."

He peered upward.

"How far up does it go?" Lovell asked. Already he was weary, his breathing labored and shallow.

"Not far," Amat said, and touched his shoulder in a comforting gesture.

But it was far. The more because Lovell could see no end to it. With the first step it seemed to be insuperable.

What they had calculated as a series of traverses back and forth across the depth of a shallow ravine that led like an inverted funnel to the top was now a cautious, silent edging upward. Now they inched along astride, on their hands, while their weapons slid down their arms to the limit of the slings; now they swung themselves off a trunk and, feeling for footing beneath, passed branches that hooked beneath pack straps or into folds of their coveralls or struck them sharply, painfully, across face and body.

Below them as they made their way there were unseen rustlings and movements. There were purposeful rushes, a scraping or slithering upon a tree bole, then sudden and utter silence, broken only by the sounds of their own progress.

Lovell fell behind farther and farther, despite Madden's intention to keep him between Amat and himself. Angry and impatient, he moved ahead finally, and Lovell, seeing the two of them disappear, roused himself to move faster, lest he lose all the advantage to be gained from watching their progress and fearing to be left alone on this desolate wooden massif.

This fear was familiar and singular, centered completely upon his present difficulties and not at all upon the future.

What lay at the top of the promontory, what could happen during the operation or the return to *Avatar*, was of no concern. What mattered now was the sight of the pack ahead of him, the back of Madden's neck, the thump of his rifle butt against a stump in this endless tortuous progress. That mattered, and his ability to maintain their pace. Nothing else.

Thankfully, it was at an end. He saw them, bent over and gasping, their legs braced against the last toppled trunk, and he took his place, gratefully, beside them.

Madden peered at his watch.

"Forty-eight minutes," he said grimly. "Forty-eight god-damn minutes."

The remark meant nothing to Lovell. It could have been twice it or ten times it. Of more importance was the racing of his heart and the bloodlessness of his face.

Then they were off again and he perforce, and under Amat's concerned eye, scrambled to his feet as well.

Now it was easier to cross the sidehill, and the darkness so impenetrable just below them concealed the terrors of a fall. Looking back and down they could see the shimmer of the sea, silent and untroubled, a refuge at the end of the affair.

They moved more quietly now, even unpracticed Lovell, placing his feet as nearly as possible where they had placed theirs. Only occasionally did they displace even clods or loose pebbles to rattle down into the chasm beneath.

Finally, at the end of the sixth traverse of the dry wash, they paused just at the military crest of the escarpment, Lovell with Madden's hand against his chest to wait until Amat reconnoitered the ground at the top.

Madden stood, one foot above the other along the elevation, and craned his neck at the crest. Lovell sat behind him, head bent, palms sweating profusely on the stock of the carbine.

"Check that piece," Madden said. "See if the barrel's clear.

"Quietly."

Lovell opened the bolt, remembering to hold his hand over the receiver to catch the ejected round, then forced it down upon the other four with his thumb and squinted, pointing the barrel at some gleam of starshine through the receiver.

He closed the bolt and put it back on safety.

The night wind blew harder up here, rustling the underbrush at the edge of the crest above them. Madden spoke again.

"Don't get killed, and don't kill anybody," he said. "That's the order. Remember."

"How many are there guarding it?" Lovell asked.

"When it went into operation, a battalion. Jeeps, an electrified fence, four towers, and two barrack huts. Then they went to a company, then a platoon. Now just militia. Nobody's ever touched it."

He leveled a finger upward.

"Mat."

It was not he, only a rustling in the undergrowth along the top of the ridge. Madden shook his head in impatience.

"Five minutes more," he said clearly in an undertone, "and we'll go without him. I don't know what happened to him, goddamn him. Maybe he's making a separate peace."

Lovell did not reply. Madden moved imperceptibly upward, inching, inching on the side of the slope, this movement the only significant indication of his impatience.

The bocage-like growth was parted, and they saw Amat against the softer dark of the sky. He leaned through and motioned them on.

At the top they paused again and peered through at an amphitheater that sloped away gently before them. Its central portion was lost in a mist so thick and gray that it obscured all but the upper sections of the two towering antenna masts.

Recalling the time on board *Avatar* when they had gone over their pictures and drawings with him during his briefing had not made this familiar to Lovell.

All the dimensions seemed mistaken to him. The deserted watchtowers roofed with sheet metal that had popped its fastenings and hung down limply like tar paper or curved sharply back—these were too small. The eight-strand barbed-wire fence was too low, its support posts leaned toward and away from them like a file of exhausted prisoners ruminating in the night, and all was softened by masses of parasitic growth that had twined itself around the wire until it looked like the beginnings of a vineyard.

Behind the fence, in the geologic sink, sugar cane grew, the stalks ranging at this season from four or five feet tall at the boundary of the fence to heights of eight or nine feet and more near Boca Grande's masts.

"Well maintained," Madden grunted.

"There's no one here," Amat said quietly. "It's deserted."

"That's ridiculous," Madden said flatly. "They're broadcasting. Did you check the power cables?"

Amat nodded.

"There aren't any. They've been removed."

"They've been buried."

"I was there," Amat said patiently. "They aren't buried, they're gone."

"It's a gimmick," Madden said. He straightened and stared into the darkness at the sea of mist, the nodding trees, the twin masts rising like cenotaphs toward the sky.

"They're waiting for us somewhere. They've been warned."

They listened beyond the sound of their own breathing. There was nothing but the breeze overhead on the rim of the basin.

"All right," Madden said finally. "So much the better. Go around and make your diversion. We'll stick to the plan."

"What for?" Amat said reasonably. He seemed at home in this place. The only one of them calm in the darkness, the silence, the absence of resistance.

He squatted on his heels, rolled a cigarette and lit it with a lighter made of an impregnated wick and a spark wheel, and smoked contemplatively, cupping the end in his large hand.

"There isn't any need to set grenades and fire the area. Just plant the charges and leave. You could take the thing down with a hacksaw."

"We can't take chances now," Madden told him. "They could come out on us in a minute when I'm setting the charges."

“Change assignments,” Amat said. “I will do it.”

“I’m not arguing,” Madden said. “We’ll do it the way we said we would before we left.”

Lovell could understand him and his insistence. The plans, the plotted, definite actions were all that was concrete in this place. Change or deviation was not possible. One would have to account for them one day.

“Bailey,” Amat told him suddenly, “this is no longer Boca Grande’s antenna. It is two towers of scrap. Meaningless. We are helping them if we take it down. It will save them the trouble.”

“Somebody’s blown the operation,” Madden said. “That’s the only way they could do this. This place was operational up to three weeks ago. Less. One of us blew it.”

“Who?” Amat said softly.

“I don’t know. But I’ll find out. After we finish here. I won’t stop until I know.”

“Do you think it could be me?”

“It could. Or Perk. Or him.” He jerked a finger at Lovell.

“You’re out of your head,” Lovell said. “You’re paranoid.”

Madden turned to him, the muzzle of his rifle pointed at the ground just between Lovell’s legs.

Lovell sensed the tension in him.

“Stay out of it,” Madden said.

Amat sighed.

“I’m the favored candidate, Bailey. Right?”

He answered himself, accurately.

“I’m the only one who could betray you and survive. I could melt into the city and surface six months from now. Or six days from now. I could have arranged it through three Malay seamen in the ship terminal in Brooklyn.

“It’s true. I could. Rightly so. There is no trust in you and no faith in anyone but you. You’re a poor kind of man who seizes events and works back to the cause to suit himself.”

He rose to his feet with dignity and glanced at his watch. "Give me ten minutes to get into position." He disappeared into the mist, across the rutted track that lay before them.

They watched him away, Madden peering after him. Then they moved, silently, placing the balls of their feet down solidly in the cane field, passing at a hundred-yard distance the first of the two towers, and on to the second.

Each mast was guyed to a concrete anchor sunk into the earth. Each supporting cable was strung to an enormous turnbuckle that terminated at an eyebolt cast in the concrete of the anchor.

Madden scrambled up to the top of the concrete cube and grunted with satisfaction.

Eyebolt and turnbuckle were at the bottom of a cylindrical hole two feet deep.

He worked with concentration, packing charges of plastic explosive around the eyebolt and turnbuckle, holed the substance with his crimping pliers, crimped two detonators tightly and snugly to the roll of orange fuse he carried, tucked the detonators into the charges, and firmed the plastic around them.

He took a hitch around the barrel of the turnbuckle with the fuse and passed the roll to Lovell to hold.

In twenty minutes he repeated this operation four times to the windward-side anchors and replaced tools, scraps, and spare detonators in the two packs.

He returned to the first two charges, fixed fuse lighters to both, and handed them to Lovell.

He glanced at his watch and nodded to himself. Having worked with neatness and dispatch, there was time in hand until Amat began his unnecessary diversion.

He crouched in the cane field and waited, silent in the mist.

There was a flare of orange red brilliance half a mile west of them. Madden counted two minutes and pulled the wires of the two fuse lighters.

He touched the fuses lightly with his index finger, then left them and withdrew to the mast nearest to their route back.

His head nodded to count the passing time.

Another of Mat's incendiaries flashed on the darkness and faded to low intense flame.

The first charge went off with a full, confined boom.

Staring at the point at which the guy wire angled upward, Lovell saw it sag, a thick curve against the two fires to the west of their position.

"Two," Madden said, bringing his hand down with definition.

The second charge sounded.

They retreated toward the fence. Madden fired the last two fuses. There was an odd expression on his face, anomalous, as though the successive blasts were an orchestration, a triumph to be followed by ovation.

Again he was counting with the fuse train. This time there was no response from the timpanum. Unbelieving, he stared at his watch and tapped its face with his fingernail.

In the time since they had come up from the sea, this silent enclave had been turned into a field of battle. The silence was breached, the dark accented by streaks and patches of ragged flame, the mist holed and dissipated by explosion.

The northernmost mast began to sway at the top. It bent suddenly, sharply, where the leeward guy wires terminated. The lower structure twisted with a grating of steel upon steel and it fell with a crash.

"Come on," Lovell said, pulling at Madden's sleeve. "Come on away. It's done."

Madden shook him off. He looked at Lovell as though uncomprehending the language.

"It's not done," he said finally. "It's not done at all. We have to finish the other one."

He took another fuse lighter from his pocket and moved forward.

"The fuse is wet. We'll reset it. Take a minute."

Lovell could see his progress against Amat's incendiaries, his head and broad shoulders as he went on, picking up the orange line of fuse, running it through both hands as he advanced toward the bulk of the concrete anchor block.

He disappeared as the side of the anchor blew out. A chunk of concrete, a corner of the block, lifted in a short arc, and settled unheard into the cane.

Lovell turned and ran for the wire, charging as though pursued. He glanced up once at the mast nearest him, head twisted, mouth wide, unable to order the sound and perception that flashed upon him.

He heard a great clang as the last guy wire snapped and the barrel of the turnbuckle struck the mast. He saw the tower twist slowly.

Then he was through the wire, his coverall ripped from knee to ankle by a long barb, and lying in the track beyond the fence, gripping the rifle with both hands and drawing it to his body as though it were a support in a sea.

When he raised his head and turned, Amat was there, crouching next to him, a hand on his shoulder.

"Can you walk?" he said. Lovell nodded, unable to speak.

Amat shook him.

"Where is he? Madden. Where is he?"

Then he disappeared into the field again and Lovell rose and moved out of the road and back onto the shoulder into the underbrush before he turned, holding the weapon at port arms, and waited.

When Amat returned he was carrying a splintered stock and the barrel and receiver of Madden's rifle.

"Not much to see," he said. "What happened?"

"He was going to reset the fuse," Lovell told him. "I tried to stop him, but I don't think he even heard me."

"Marching to a different drum," Amat said. "He never heard anybody. The right man in the wrong place at the wrong time."

He sat down, seemingly exhausted.

"I can't even pity him. That's what he leaves behind. That and the wish that I could be like him and live in that world that has proper order. Where fuses burn six feet to the second. Where all the plans are correct and want only the right men to carry them out.

"Now he's with the heroes." He rubbed his forehead. "And I am left.

"Listen," he said to Lovell, "you can get back yourself, can't you? I'll go with you down the trees, but you can go on from there, right?

"I have to salvage what I can from this, for myself. If I don't draw them off—look," he added, and pointed off down the escarpment.

There was a wink of successive light, like an occulting buoy there.

"How much time is there?" Lovell asked. "They're far away. An hour or maybe two."

"I don't think so," Amat said. He grinned. "They drive like maniacs. They'll lose two jeeps on the way, but they'll be here in less than that time.

"If there is someone with brains leading, they will start throwing shells all over our beach and out to sea.

"And they do have brains. Come on."

He led the way below the crest and took the descending traverses more steeply, side-slipping in a controlled slide like a skier. At the first of the tangled stumps and tree boles, he halted.

He handed Lovell his watch and pocket compass.

"Give me the rifle," he said, and slung it across his back. He transferred his own pack to Lovell's back. It was all done without urgency, quickly, efficiently, with little waste motion.

"Be sure you sink everything. Don't try to keep the receiver or transmitter he had. That will keep you out of it even if you are stopped."

He shook his head sadly.

"You have Perkinson to show them. Madden—me—you know better than I what to say. We went over the side in the same accident. Perkinson's proof. Agh."

He gestured.

"Someone will meet you at Jamaica. Tell him I have no plan but that I'll be useful."

He smiled suddenly, brightly.

"That's the story of my life. Right?"

He held out his hand and Lovell took it.

"Happier voyages," he said, and he turned quickly and climbed away to the top of the escarpment. Lovell could see him clearly as he moved up, tirelessly, toward the soft red glow above.

"How do we know our revolution is a success? The
Committee for the Defense of the Revolution tells us:
Five hundred thousand new members have enrolled
for a new total of four point five million members.
Seven thousand seven hundred and fifty-nine regular
committee branches have been formed. A monthly
average of two million three hundred and thirty-five
thousand members attend our meetings."

BOCA GRANDE 3 / 15

Lovell began the climb down very differently. Fear and the hurry to be away from here, and even a haphazard familiarity with its difficulties, helped his progress. There were the occulting flashes again, nearer this time too, but there was also the knowledge that there was no choice.

He accepted whiplashing branch, the sudden gouge of a broken limb, the harrowing moment when he misplaced his foot and fell an unknown distance. He landed with a thud on hands and knees, thankfully, on a broad stump canted at an angle, and went on without a pause.

Finally he was down, pained and breathless. He sprawled full length while the seconds ticked away until he could breathe normally again.

He was disoriented for a brief time and unable to find the dinghy. Two tries he made and then in panic turned to run to the beach. The thought of swimming out and out halted him instantly and he looked again, controlled, and found it.

He pulled the two $CO_2$ lanyards and inflated it and towed it with the two packs through lanai grass and down to the beach.

His watch read 0240 hours. The time and the dinghy, Amat above him, and the advancing blinking lights far to the west were all that were real. Even the sea itself he saw as though dreaming, the gentle successive waves, curving with foam apart from the black expanse beyond.

There could be no boat out there.

He dragged the dinghy off in a hushed rubbing of sand and marched it through the shallows. He rolled into it when the warmth of the sea reached his waist and, lying at length with his chin resting on the front of it, swam it offshore, pulling with both hands in a tiring breaststroke.

Once under way, aided by the tide, he could keep it moving, gaining yards at a stroke, the headway satisfying, putting distance between himself and the beach.

Offshore he heard the flat, unmistakable whack of the carbine, the five rounds in its clip spaced as if aimed with care.

Then there was the slam of the submachine gun. He could hear the heavy bolt working. It was fired in short bursts, expertly, two and three rounds at a time, as though someone were firing cover for an advance.

The same sequence was repeated again, and yet a third time before there was an answer.

When the response came, it was overwhelming, and from automatic weapons. Looking back and up toward the top of the escarpment, Lovell could pick out the sudden tongues of flame and, dimly, shouts and directions when the firing ceased.

He heard Amat's weapons again, this time farther away, toward the east, their distinctiveness lost in the counterfire.

Then the vehicles were moving again, following on, beating the darkness before them.

Lovell turned back to his task, the action hidden from him by a turn of the shore, moving through the warm and phosphorescing sea.

He went on for a time, steadily, keeping himself under control, pacing himself, aware of his waning strength. He was sure that he had worked for half an hour.

Twelve minutes by the watch.

But he could feel a difference in the tide and the presence of a current. Perhaps it was only a rip over uneven bottom.

He lay still, his head hanging down before the dinghy, mouth gaping, arms at his sides. He longed to stay there, just so, abiding, until sleep came.

He saw himself in the sunrise, with the tide on the turn, alone on the surface of the bright sea, carried back, back, while his strength dissipated, finally, to that same shore.

This time there would be someone waiting.

Then he heard them, the same rattle of sheet blocks and winch that he had heard when they had dropped off *Avatar* five hours before.

Kneeling, he listened like an alerted dog and stared into the soft night, controlled, peering into the southwest quadrant and the southeast with tiny movements of his chin to mark the place. His eyes watered with the staring and he saw the glimmer of topside against the blackness. He fell back into position and stroked toward them, yard by frenzied yard, hoping that he would have breath to shout when he was close enough, and that the shout would not be lost in the grind of winch and the noise on board.

He could see the mast, towering against the paler sky, and hear the flap of the mainsail, untended.

"Here!" he shouted suddenly. "Here!"

Ten strokes, and ten more, and he was alongside. Max and

Iacovino dragged him aboard and tumbled him into the cockpit. He lay on his back and stared up at them. Colleran peered down from the wheel, for minutes it seemed, before he spun the spokes and put the boat about with an agonizing loss of more time, more time.

He braced his foot against lee side, as though now he would feel a surge as it gathered way, and heeled at eight knots and more.

There was no surge, only the slatting of the sail and a faint motion of the boom above him.

"Sail it," he whispered hoarsely. "Sail it off."

"We are," Max told him, "we're moving. The breeze is out a bit."

"What happened?" Iacovino asked. "Shit hit the fan?"

He dropped down and put a cushion under Lovell's head.

"You want a drink, right?"

He nodded.

"All around."

He disappeared into the cabin and reached out the brandy bottle.

Lovell drank deeply and shoved himself into a sitting position.

They seemed to be moving a little faster, Colleran peering tensely forward, taking the genoa sheet in inches at a time, as the breeze filled breath by breath, sailing from cat's-paw to cat's-paw, maintaining his helmsman's discipline.

Iacovino gave him a cup of coffee, heavily sugared as he himself liked it.

While he drank it they spoke to him quietly and he told them what had happened.

"How's Perkinson?" he said suddenly.

"Bad," Max told him. "Bad." He gazed at his fingertips. "We can't do anything. Must be a lot of pressure on his brain now," he said, clinically, calmly.

Lovell looked back over the stern. They were far enough out now so that the bulk of the island came defined. There was a glimmer of orange, half up the height of it. Perhaps where Boca Grande lay. Then that was gone.

Iacovino relieved Colleran at the wheel.

"Come on," he said. "I can steer in this kind of breeze."

It had freshened steadily as they moved offshore. There was the sound of waves under the forefoot and the sails curved in finite shapes.

"Two-ten," Colleran said, and logged the change of helmsman.

"He's been on the wheel since you left," Iacovino said. "Except for a piss call off the backstay."

"Thanks," Lovell said simply. Colleran nodded.

"*Nada,*" he said, and sat down opposite.

"You're beat," he said sympathetically.

Lovell nodded, licking the salt from his lips, conscious of every year of his age.

He had stripped off his coveralls and his sneakers and he looked down at himself, the muscles in his shoulders and arms still twitching, leaping under the skin, uncontrollable, still reacting to the desperate flight down and back from there.

"I didn't think about either of them, Frank," he said quietly. "Amat told me to go and I ran. Fast. I didn't even go and look at Madden, poor bastard."

"Who would?" Iacovino said from the wheel.

"I would have. Once," Lovell said. He shivered suddenly, rose quickly, and went below. Perkinson lay on the double bunk. Lovell glanced at him as he went forward to his sea bag.

His face had fallen in upon the bones beneath it. His nose beaked sharply at the bridge. His breathing was harsh and stertorous, and a thin line of blood ran from the deep line at the corner of the nostril to his mouth.

Lovell found a pair of sailing shorts and a baggy sweater and put them on. The sweater hung from his shoulders, concealing his thickened waist. He went on deck again, in a compulsion to talk more.

They had been speaking quietly, but the instant his head appeared in the hatch they were silent, waiting, refining what they would have to say, each wearing an impersonal mask, hoping to disguise their interest in what he would reveal—the center of the man.

Lovell looked at them and smiled grimly.

"You look like a priest," he said to Max.

"I should," Max said. "He was a forebear of mine, not theirs."

"What surprises me most," Lovell said conversationally, "was my fear. It just encompassed me. Flooded me. Did you ever have a time when that happened to you?"

"You don't have to tell us anything," Iacovino said. "Wait until you've had a sleep. Talk about it then."

Colleran gestured him to silence, but he would not accept it.

"Come on, cut it out," Iacovino insisted. "Let him alone. Whatever he tells you now, he'll regret."

"If he wants to talk, let him talk," Max said. "Fuck off. We're doing him a favor. Can't you see that?"

"That's a lot of shit," Iacovino said. "The same as when that Swede drowned and we told each other how great we were. Seamen. Great seamen."

"Two things bother me," Lovell said quietly. "More than two, actually, because I always thought of myself as a good man. When I thought about it at all. But I don't seem to be. Do I?"

The three of them immediately donned expressions that indicated doubt, but very little.

"I don't think I care. Not now. Anyhow, this is what I've done—adultered, right; used my friends, corrupted myself, wrecked my family and future, left a comrade to die—"

"They won't kill him. They won't even catch him," Max said. "We talked about this very situation one night. He told me he had one great ability—he could survive anywhere. Honestly, I remember almost every word."

"Fine," Lovell said. "But that's what I've done and that's what I am. Me. And I'm part of the top of the society.

"Remember something else too—I didn't go into this because I'm a supporter of government or I believed in the mission either. Just good old venality. And don't forget him."

He gestured toward the cabin.

"How's that for decency?"

"I'm letting my other friend die in his own shit."

Colleran shook his head angrily.

"Not so. Not so. Max has seen to that, and Amat before he went ashore.

"We can't give you absolution. You have to find your own way. But you're not objective at all. There's been a good thing or two happen, and evil as you think you are, that's in your favor.

"We behaved like men when we had to. We took care of Perkinson and came back to get you. We could see the shooting on the cliff. If you hadn't been there and we hadn't got you, I don't know whether we'd have stayed until dawn or come back again either. I'm glad we didn't have to decide. But there's something there. Don't doubt that.

"Listen, John, the rest of us are small men too. Wee men, the Irish say. No giants. 'Coward take my coward's hand.'

"We only have so much principle and idealism—just as we've only got so much brain and so much bicep, so much stamina. You've got more than some and not as much as others."

Lovell stared at him, frowning, comforted and quieter; the words passed between them like an unguent. He tried to remember them in sequence.

Now he could sleep. He went forward into the forepeak and stretched himself flat upon the berth. He turned his hands to his cheek and was asleep.

When he awoke it was after sunrise, the boat moving swiftly, deeper on the same tack, a broader reach, and he could not see the boom end when he peered down the length of her and out into the cockpit.

Colleran was on the wheel again and Lovell could see the strain of the night on his face.

Lovell drew some water at the sink, washed his face quickly, and brushed his teeth. Carefully he avoided looking at Perkinson, but the sound of his breathing—unrhythmic, irregular—was there.

Out of habit, he wiped the galley sink and cleaned his plastic cup and put it back on the shelf. On deck, Max leaned against the mast and aimed his sextant at the sun.

Iacovino sat forward on the high side.

"Where's the dinghy?" Lovell said.

"Cast it off last night," Colleran told him. "It was like a sea anchor. We took the packs out. Put 'em in that lazaret."

"Did you sink it?"

Colleran shook his head.

"That was the last thing Amat told me to do. Sink it."

"We didn't leave anything in it," Max said.

"Fine," Lovell told him. "Good enough."

He took the packs from the lazaret and went through them. Part of a roll of fuse, extra lighters. The spare detonators were gone and the grenades. The map was there and the photographs of Boca Grande, a small camera, four or five pounds of gray plastic explosive, and the transistor board that Madden had removed from the standard transmitter.

He put everything but that back in them, went forward and gathered up Madden's special transmitter and its batteries, the rest of the photographs and all the special charts. He forced all this into the two packs as well, and weighed them judiciously in his arms.

He went below again, this time to the forecabin, and picked up the cabin sole planks and removed two ballast pigs from the bilge.

These he dropped in each pack, laced them together with their own straps, and dropped them over the side, impassively.

In ten minutes Max reported their position.

"It's not a good angle," he said, "but it's pretty close."

They were almost fifty miles offshore and moving at better than seven knots.

"I'll relieve you," he told Colleran, and took his place on the wheel.

He logged the change, the log book open, pages flipping in the breeze, reading with a hint of a smile the earlier entries:

"Took departure from Blighty-under-the-Palms. Pass Committee Boat Close Aboard. Ladies also have mustaches and stiff lips."

"Telephone number in Jamaica printed across belly button in magic marker. Note: bikini is zebra-striped in black and orange. Ask for Deirdre, if first in fleet. Obviously planted by Skipper."

"Message received and contents noted."

"Ship and crew in good order save for certain bowels."

"Recommend quinine water on cornflakes as cure for constipation."

"Will accept remedy when level reaches soft palate."

"You know, John," Max said from the cabin hatch, "we had planned that if we didn't pick you up last night we were going to put out a Mayday. For Perkinson. We had a bad case of nerves then, after we dropped you off. He was very bad—the way he was just after it happened. We began to come apart. Couldn't keep him quiet. There we were feeling our way inshore after you and he began to talk again. Clearly."

"It must have been pretty awful," Lovell said. "Put it out now."

"I can't. The part that Madden took out is still missing."

Lovell took it from his pocket and handed it to him. A bit of circuitry.

Max looked at it and shook his head.

"I guess he was right not to trust us. That was perceptive of him."

"Very," Lovell said. "And hoist the ensign. Upside down too. Can't hurt. And the radar reflector."

"Won't help much," Iacovino said. He took the bright ensign out of the flag locker and raised it to the spreader.

Lovell switched on the engine and ran it for fifteen minutes. It started without hesitation. Another contribution from Jensen.

Max issued a general call for assistance. Then he switched to the race frequency and called again.

All around them there was nothing to be seen under the blue of the sky. The surface of the sea was ruffled by the steady breeze and lay empty of ships, but the response was almost immediate.

They were no longer alone.

Voices sounded on the speaker. They seemed concerned, sympathetic, through the flat impersonality of the transmissions.

A French cruise liner responded, indicating its position a hundred miles to the west, and offered to put its doctor on stand-by for instruction in treatment.

A plane came in to suggest contact with the nearest airport so that a helicopter could be dispatched.

A competitor in the race with a doctor in the crew asked for *Avatar*'s heading and proposed to turn back and meet her and announced the time it would calculate as necessary.

Max was writing down call signs in haste.

"Sounds like a message center," Colleran said, and went to help.

A more incisive voice came in.

"This is a priority transmission," it stated, as though to accept neither delay nor competition.

"Western Caribbean Assistance Patrol," it continued. "How do you read me?"

"Clear," Max said. "Loud and clear."

"Accept responsibility to provide all required aid to you. Switch to the following frequency." The voice repeated it twice and Max tuned to it.

WCAP, as it announced itself, set forth a detailed program.

Instructions for the care of Perkinson until their surface vessel could reach *Avatar* sounded much like what they had read from their own first-aid manual.

But it corresponded so closely with what they had done for him that it seemed to confirm the treatment they had given. The reassurance was satisfying.

They were also exact with their plot. They required two hours to rendezvous. *Avatar* needed only to maintain her course.

"End transmission. Monitor this frequency every fifteen minutes," the voice added, and was silent.

They bettered their estimated time of arrival by thirty minutes.

Iacovino spotted them off the bow. First a tiny splash on the horizon in the distance, then a shape, finally a color, very difficult to pick out on the blue of the seas.

"Some color for a rescue boat," Colleran remarked.

They closed the last miles in a rush, a thirty-footer with an open stern. There was a ring mount around the hatch far forward and a crew of four, very suntanned and wearing khakis and peaked caps.

Lovell brought *Avatar* up into the wind and held her there, rolling in the seas. Both crews put fenders over and made fast.

Their captain came on board as soon as the gap between them could be negotiated, looked them all over in turn, and asked for the injured man.

Colleran stood by the wheel and Lovell went below with him.

He wasted no time in talking.

Two of his men passed over a basket stretcher and followed it.

Gently they maneuvered Perkinson into it and into the stern of their own vessel, then forward, opposite the wheel.

"You're Lovell," the captain said. "Name is Mackey. If you can, we'd like you to come. Give the details. Your crew can manage to bring the boat in, or would you like me to leave one or two of mine?"

"Let's go," Lovell said, boarding.

"If it's not against the rules," Mackey said to Colleran, "your finish line is sixty-eight miles ahead, course two-two-one."

"We'll cross," Colleran said, "but it won't matter, I'm sure."

He waved and, freed from the other, *Avatar* eased away downwind.

The other boat's engine roared low and accelerated steadily to twenty knots, twenty-five, the helmsman picking his way as carefully as possible at such a speed.

"That's not the greatest for him, is it?" Lovell said, gesturing toward Perkinson.

"Half speed's not much better," Mackey said, "and takes twice the time.

"Watch your helm," he added, and indicated a seat in the stern to Lovell.

"Beer?" he shouted over the engines.

Lovell shook his head.

"Where are the other two?" he bellowed.

"What other two?"

Mackey nodded.

"It'll keep!" he said.

He went forward to stand beside the helmsman, balancing against the thumping, pulsing movement.

Lovell sat in a private limbo, watching the bow wave curl away in a rhythm, a mysterious progression of height and of sound—three, four, eight at deck level with a corresponding thud, and then another at bridge height, a sheet of water, an ephemeral rainbow, and a sudden heavy shock.

He counted away, occupied, working at the progression, worrying it, as though the solution would marshal all of past times into even, successive occurrences.

Mackey was shouting at him, pointing to port.

"Montego Bay!"

Lovell nodded.

They turned inshore in a broad sweeping arc to the west of where Mackey had pointed.

Twenty minutes later the helmsman eased the throttles. The bow settled gently into the seas. They purred ahead past the one-hundred-fathom curve, sharply defined here in the color of the water, and on inshore to a substantial concrete pier where two other craft painted the same indefinite pale blue were moored.

There was a large sign at the end of the dock.

"Light Cove Colony. Private Dock. Members and Guests Only."

The Light Cove facilities resembled every tourist folder that Lovell had ever seen and most of the ones that he had visited from Acapulco to Nassau.

There was a scattering of thatched-roof bungalows, comfortably washed in blue or white with brightly enameled doors suitably isolated from each other. A main building was set in a palm grove. There was a rank of sunfish, rigged, lying at the water's edge. There was a long bar facing the water with a dozen brightly painted stools drawn up to it. There was the green cyclone fence that surrounded the tennis courts farther away in the grove. Just before the wide white staircase that led to the main house there was a pool, sparkling blue and furnished with mats upholstered in prints that matched the hibiscus and bougainvillaea, the geraniums and oleander that bloomed in tubs and plantings all around.

It was very tasteful, very expensive, and quite deserted, as though the company in residence had decided to leave en masse.

"Where's the hospital?" Lovell asked. Mackey supervised the transfer of Perkinson to the back of a jeep tricked out in painted peace flowers on blushing pink.

"Stateside," Mackey told him. "If you want to say good-bye, he'll be there in three hours. He needs a neurosurgeon and facilities."

Lovell took Perkinson's flaccid hand and pressed it hard, as though his own quickness could be shared out between them.

Perkinson opened one eye and the other lid fluttered with the effort he made.

One corner of his mouth turned down in a hard firm line, but his lips moved and he spoke. Lovell bent down toward him with that elaborate calmness that is there when visiting the ill.

"Poo," he said. "Poo formance. Back 'ough. Main thing."

Lovell nodded.

"Not so poor. But we're back. Everthing's fine now. Just fine."

The jeep went into gear and rolled away up the shelled path from the pier, past the grove, and out of sight.

"Say," Mackey said heartily, as though the thought had just

occurred to him, "why don't you just whip into 'Ottilie' over there and clean up. I can lend you some clothes, if you like."

"Ottilie?"

"Cottage. The one with the blue door. 'Regine' has yellow, 'Mamre' is orange. The manager named them. Bartlett. He'll be down to see you after a while."

"Sure," Lovell said, "lend me some clothes." He felt his furred face. "And a razor."

"All in there," Mackey said. "Use what you need. Make yourself at home. What size's your waist?"

"Thirty-six. I could get into thirty-four."

"No problem," Mackey said cheerfully. "You go ahead, I'll toss them through the door."

Despite its name, its bright drapes, its carpet and its flowered bedspreads, Ottilie was depressing. There was no evidence that it had ever been used by another human. All its accouterments, from wastebasket to soap cakes and fluffy towels, were dustless and seemed to have been deposited there by a sensitive machine.

In an hour he was at the bar near the beach wearing a bright yellow shirt and a pair of pale green sailing shorts. They did not seem to be Mackey's taste at all.

A young black behind the bar was shaking the last drops of a bacardi into a chilled coupe. Lovell's mouth watered.

The barman nodded to Lovell.

"Make it two?" he asked, and his solitary customer turned on the barstool and held out his hand.

"Hello, Captain," he said. "Bill Bartlett. Manager here."

"Stir up another? Or would you rather have something else?"

"A daiquiri," Lovell said.

"Good," Bartlett said solemnly. "We have a rum that's really special.

"So," he said quietly, "you people had a difficult time. Too bad. When did things go wrong?"

“Who are you?” Lovell said tiredly. “What is Light Cove Colony, and the Western Caribbean Assistance Patrol?”

“Subsidiaries,” Bartlett told him. “Supportive subsidiaries. We handle details when things don’t go as planned. Do the debriefing. Restore flagging spirits. Set the backup in motion.

“We’ll see that *Avatar* is berthed and the rest of the crew is accommodated and their transportation arranged.

“We’ll put out an explanation to the race committee. We’ll see what sort of help you can give us with our backup.”

“I can’t tell you very much,” Lovell said. “What I saw and did. What happened to Perkinson. I did see that clearly.”

The barman set Lovell’s drink down and waited without interest for a comment.

Lovell nodded and sipped.

“Life,” Bartlett said.

He placed the microphone of a tape recorder between them.

“That was sad,” he said, taking out a note pad and dating the sheet at the top, “but it has a low priority at the moment.

“These things happen. Sometimes the simplest operations turn out to be very complex. Sanguinary.”

“This one certainly was,” Lovell said. “A one hundred per cent casualty rate.”

“That’s what I said—sanguinary.”

“Madden was. He surely was.”

“Is he dead? Observed to be dead by you personally?” Bartlett asked, almost idly. He had a remarkable repertory of shrugs, hunchings, and hand, finger, and arm gestures that he employed, as though they added emphasis to his questions and would help Lovell to recall specific situations in more detail.

He waved his downturned palm at the flagstones beneath the barstools in a symbolic movement that flattened Madden to the eternal earth.

"I didn't look at him. Amat did. He took his pack and what was left of his weapon."

"Which was?" Bartlett prompted, raising his fingers and cupping them upon an imaginary rifle foregrip.

"A rifle. Or . . . no. The carbine. Amat brought back just the stock. Splintered."

"Which was it? Rifle or carbine?"

"How the hell do I remember?"

"It's important. It has to do with your accuracy and your credibility. You learned that a long time ago, didn't you?"

"All right," Lovell conceded. "I think we changed weapons on the way up. I was taking the rifle, and when we started worming our way up that ravine full of logs or tree trunks, the butt was slipping all over the place and it bounced once and hit me in the balls.

"Genitals," he repeated closer to the microphone.

He halted, remembering the sudden pain.

"I swore, fairly loud, and Madden got angry and took the rifle and gave me the carbine. It was smaller and lighter. I could manage that okay."

"Then you changed back again."

"Right. At the top."

"Those tree trunks you mentioned—that was your exact route to the top where they had been flung?"

"I think so."

"You aren't certain? Did they check their strip map and co-ordinates?"

"Yes. Amat handled that. He had a compass. I saw him do that."

"Why did they take that route up, if it was so difficult?"

"Don't know."

He drew from Lovell the recollected journey up the cliff-side and into the cane field and down again, withdrawing flashes of detail that he himself had not known that he knew.

Lovell worked away at the task, sipping his drink, steadily freshened or replaced, prompted by the gestures and the quiet interest to vividness. If he expressed anger or political opinions, Bartlett did not interrupt or oppose.

When he had finished they listened together like kinsmen to what they had taped.

"Once more?" Bartlett asked, holding up his index finger.

Lovell nodded. Again the tape ran.

Listening, Lovell was aware of a sense of unease.

Certainly it was what had happened to him. It was the truth to the best of his recollection. But there was a theme that was disturbing in it, the emergence of a character and a presence that had dominated the whole circumstance.

"Something you want to add to it?" Bartlett said equably.

"I don't know," Lovell said, frowning. "It's my statement, but it doesn't say what I expected it to. Or it's different, somehow."

Bartlett shook his head.

"What's developed is a problem that I don't think you were aware of at the time. You couldn't be. You didn't have all the facts at your disposal that we did.

"That was essentially a very simple straightforward operation. Now it's failed and two valuable men were lost."

"Three," Lovell said.

"Two. Perkinson and Madden. The third is alive and well, and outside our reach. By your testimony."

Affected, Lovell held up his own hand and turned his head away.

"Just a minute. You're saying my statement is proof that your operation was sabotaged by Amat."

"Never," Bartlett told him. "You have no part in this beyond what you've done and the statement you've given. It's not proof. It's merely part of the analysis we have to do.

"We've invested time, money, and good personnel, and we

are accountable for those things. We don't just say 'tough shit' and walk away.

"Why would we?"

"When I left Amat," Lovell said reasonably, "I told you what he said—that he would be useful. That was his message—I imagine to you."

"What would you expect him to say—'I'm where I wanted to be all the time'?"

"I know speciousness when I hear it. All you're doing is taking one fact—that he remained there—and working back from there and using me to fortify a weak hypothesis."

"Board of inquiry will decide that," Bartlett said, and he rose to his feet and gathered his papers and his tape recorder together.

He looked at his watch.

"Look," he said, "there'll be gossip in the racing fleet about you losing three men, and I imagine the race committee will try and go into it.

"I can have you and your crew on a plane to New York late this afternoon and that will spare you that. Do you want to stay and explain or get drunk or what?"

"Explain to who? I don't give a goddamn about anything but what you're developing about Amat."

Bartlett shuffled his notes together into a stack and looked over Lovell's head at the pale shallows behind him.

"Half of this work is thesis," Bartlett said, frowning and shaping a simple form with his hands. "Our information in that area is supposed to be current—less than twenty-four hours old if need be. Yet your route up is choked with logs. The antenna is inoperative. The two platoons of militia are not there but there is a mobile counterforce available an hour away. A staple piece of fuse, lab-tested for burning rate even under water, is defective and costs us a middle-level man.

"This is not presumption. This is fact. Those facts state other facts: our Order of Battle information for that stretch of coast is inaccurate; our informant net for the area is lazy, incompetent, or AC-DC; our materiel is dated, or unreliable; one of our knowledgeable people is adrift in the area, unsupervised and out of contact.

"In a border state where we had every advantage—proximity, special acquaintanceship, freedom of movement. This is not Thailand, or Ghana.

"Your part in the affair is over. We'll take statements from your crew and read your log, and we want everything on board left as is.

"That bell-fitting that broke—do you still have it?"

"I think so. I don't know. I think someone taped it over so that it wouldn't foul or cut the halliards."

"We'll want to analyze that and see what caused it to fail.

"You know," he said pensively, "there's never any clarity. Never a beginning and never an end. Just continuity—a continuousness like one of those roads in a children's book. The land is there—the countryside—but you never see where the giant lives or how the ogre got to set up under the bridge.

"Well," he added briskly, "let me know when you want to go back and I'll arrange it."

Lovell drained his glass. The bartender made him another. He took it with him to a long chair under the palms near the sea.

He tipped his sunglasses down and stared out across the quiet cove and back to the north and east across the water and beyond.

He cast about for the reasons he had come.

"It must have been an image," he said aloud. "A captain with a knowing hand on the tiller. Venturing out."

He laughed aloud.

"I wouldn't have done it for any other payment. Would I?"

He conned his susceptibility and aligned all his reasons in order. They were demeaning.

He returned quickly to the bar.

"I want to go back," he said to the barman. "Ask Bartlett to fix it for me—as soon as he can."

"On the occasion of the opening day of operation of this great new marvel of communications, this new sound of freedom on the planet, let us together raise our voices in a single cry of faith and hope! Shout with me so it will be heard through ethereal, infinite space!"

BOCA GRANDE 4/1

There was a sense of completion and an affirmation of the
Coming home was comforting.
existence of ties. He did not permit himself to consider how much he deserved to have them.

He had served for years and they owed him the hugs and handshakes, smiles and comforts.

They were early for his train next morning, and Joyce looked at him obliquely as she moved over behind the wheel.

She said, "Did you find what you were looking for? I'm not being nasty. I'm interested."

"No," he said shortly. "I don't think so. Is there time to talk about it now?"

"We'll make an appointment to do it," Joyce told him. She softened the statement with a warm smile.

He kissed her and walked away past the spring plantings in the station garden. This morning in late March there was the sense of greenness in the grass plots and about the privet and maples, an aura of promised leaf.

In his office the mail was stacked in the order of its delivery. Each piece that had been opened had been initialed by the opener. There was a haphazard stack of memoranda from Ray and others to inform him of what had occurred in his absence.

Ray came into his office at ten-thirty and shook hands perfunctorily.

"Listen," he said without preliminary, "they were talking about you the other night at the club. Goddamnedest stories I ever heard. Said you'd lost three men. That true?"

Lovell nodded.

"What else did they say?"

"I don't know. Sounded like garbage to me. There was an objectionable child there—the Lillis kid had just got back that afternoon. Said there was a real stink and that the race committee wanted a full-scale inquiry. Said you didn't appear and had got a local lawyer to sneak you out of the country."

"What else?"

Ray looked at him. He sat down in the armchair that matched the leather couch near the bookshelves where Lovell kept Joshua Slocum; *The History of the Coast Watchers in America;* Hakluyt; Captain Voss in a corner of the lowest shelf, the remaining shelf space ranked with an overflow of torts and jurisprudences from their library.

"He was lurid," Ray said. "I'm enough of a lawyer to know that what he said was mostly crap, but it's the kind of tale that people chew on. Probably because the goddamn sport is so dull.

"Long stretches where a gull dropping a load on someone's head is an event.

"The point is, you're the point. Your crew wasn't reliable. Your boat was barely qualified. You were inexperienced. You had a bad racing record."

"You say anything?" Lovell asked.

Ray shrugged.

"I had nothing to say. It was the first I'd heard about it."

"Do you believe it?"

"As your friend or your boss or what?"

"As someone who knows me well. There aren't many who know me better."

"I don't know you very well at all," Ray said. There was a stoniness to him, calculated, quiet, controlled.

"Like what you did with Constance, for example. That was a surprise to me. She told me about it."

Lovell looked down at the pile of memos and mail on the desk top.

The statement settled in the center of his mind: "What you did with Constance." He had a terrible desire to laugh. The corners of his mouth pursed and he stared at Ray, who had pinched and prodded and played his way along, and thought of an answer. "Nothing you wouldn't see the baboons do in the zoo, Gray Ray."

"Ray," he said, "do you remember the night we were in Chicago and you picked up that cocktail waitress, the one with the big breasts, and the two of us took her way the hell out to—where was it?—Joliet or near there in a cab?"

"No," Ray said, "I don't.

"And I don't like your goddamn comparison. So leave it right there. In the first place, I don't have to justify what I do to you."

"But I do to you."

"Mine was a goddamn aberration. If it ever happened. Yours was a betrayal. It was an amoral act."

"I thought it was love," Lovell said simply.

Ray stood up, his fury apparent.

"You'll never get another chance to play cynic with me," he said. "There are some things that you aren't going to debase. You're like a goddamn infant. You don't have the maturity to understand the relationship, so it has no value. Better go someplace and think about it awhile."

"It's all right," Lovell told him generously. "You have a right to be angry. But I'm not being cynical. I meant it."

He wanted to go on. He wanted to speak more of Constance to him. He tried delicately to do so. But it could not be done. His attempts met only more anger, more distaste, more choler.

Stating the level of his own feeling for her only inflamed Ray the more. As though Lovell were a martyr, his course toward sainthood charted; as though he were appearing before a base inquisitor.

Ray leaned across the desk toward him.

"Presumption is your whole character. In small ways most men don't even think of—and some of them are contemptible, my friend.

"I wouldn't mind so much if you didn't presume your appreciation for my wife is nobler, or that you're more principled, or more honorable than I am. You're arrogant in circumstances where there's one judgment possible: disgusting!"

Lovell responded, pushing himself at long last down the path to disaster, drawn to it by years of quiescence.

He was like a man who lives near a crevasse and visits it periodically. Occasionally he tests the depth with a pebble. A man who will hold one foot over its edge to experience the half of disaster.

He did not choose a phrase that would have left both feet in the air.

He did not say, as he had heard Ray say to an accountant

who stuttered so when in Ray's presence that every comment took minutes, "Squeeze it out, man, say it." And Ray would grunt as though moving his bowels.

Lovell assumed as pained and concerned an expression as he could manage. "What's the solution, Ray?" he asked.

"I don't know," he muttered.

"Why don't you throw me out?" Lovell asked tiredly.

"Goddamn if I know," Ray said, and he left, going out into the unnaturally silent corridor.

Lovell did not go out to lunch. He was unwilling to risk awkwardness in the lobby while waiting for an elevator. Instead he went on through the mail. It was a collection of seductions that promised education, increased abilities, more culture, more services, more and simpler ways to make money at no risk. There was also more protection available for his family, for himself, for his house, his car, his boat, his office.

He read it religiously until two-thirty.

Then he went home and stayed there for two days. They closed ranks around him. Nancy and Jack brought him small tales of their achievements and assured him that they would never have occurred without his influence. They were serious and circumspect.

When he returned to the office there was a manila folder on his desk—the semiannual "Review of Personnel Compensation"—across which Ray had scrawled "FYI" and "Need this soonest."

He opened it and went back to work.

Two weeks later he took Joyce to Provincetown for a long weekend.

They had not been up there in years. Just before spring the town was almost deserted, the motels still shuttered against the sand-blasting winds of winter.

Along the main street the last remnants of a black, crusted snow were still evident.

He stopped at the dock where three or four trawlers and two local lobster boats were moored.

One of the men gave him the name of a woman who took an occasional tourist all year round. He turned the car around and drove back to the place.

Whenever they traveled with the children, it was Joyce who searched out the accommodation, she who fixed the price, she who called for whatever services they required.

Now, she leaned her head against the rest and closed her eyes.

"You do it," she said.

There was a room—bright and airy and facing the setting sun, with a feather bed covered in calico patches. The woman was casual and pleasant and told them she was happy to have company.

He brought a bottle down and asked her to have a drink with them.

She led the way into her tiny bar, tacked onto the house. It was a glassed-in wooden platform on pilings twenty feet above the water. They sat at one of the corner tables and watched the sun, cold and pale, lower toward the sea.

The room was a pleasant one and furnished without the gimcrackery that so many such places affect. The duck decoys were carved—some not well, but serviceably. They would remain upright in a wind. The net floats looked as though they had been retrieved from the sea.

She chatted with them long enough and told them which restaurant to go to of the two that were open and the proper size lobster to order.

Then she left them to themselves, refusing a second drink.

He raised his glass.

"Monogamy," he said. Joyce smiled and did not respond.

"Not a bad place to be," he said. "What would you think if I took a new job for which I am qualified?"

"What?"

"Lighthouse keeper. All you have to know is how to row and wash glass."

He was aware of how much she did not know about him. Now he set himself to find out how much she did know. But she forestalled him quickly.

"You're a poorly made man," she told him, "but you're not very different from the others.

"All those conversations that go on endlessly between and among women aren't about recipes, you know, don't you? If you don't, you should."

"What are they about?"

"Men."

She stared across the quiet bay, unwilling to stake her knowledge, realizing that a mistake in detail would be an indication that she was only speculating. She turned back to him abruptly.

"Nobody's ever challenged me over the years either. I live an automated life. I respond to the things that are supposed to be important. I'm not committed to them. Screw braces and drunken socializing and whether the school's going downhill and the neighborhood too.

"If you just weren't so goddamn certain that you're the only one who sees our life in a bad light, I'd agree with you.

"You associate me with your dissatisfaction. And I can't convince you that it's not so, and I make myself a real symbol for you. Don't I?"

"I think so."

"Well, then, I'm going to show you what a wife is for. A good one. A good woman. I don't care who you screwed or when or how often. I do, but I don't. I will call it an overdose of romanticism.

"As for the rest of it, you're no man who would leave three

others to drown, and if anybody says it in my presence or even alludes to it, I'll punch them."

She flourished her fist and he smiled.

"Put your thumb on the outside," he told her, "otherwise you'll break it."

He took her arm, and their bottle, and raised her to her feet.

"Come on," he said, "let's see what that feather bed has to offer."

Saturday morning he drove to Dennis and found the Perkinson place. He passed it twice, the entrance between two tumble-down stone pillars almost concealed by a thick growth of old wisteria.

It was a cottage of a kind one might see on a promontory on the Cornish coast—slate-roofed, with the peaks at the gable perked perceptibly upward.

Perkinson's wife met him at the door, her voice as soft and pleasing as it had been on the phone. There was a sense of the withdrawn about her in person, strength, and competence, but aloofness as well, as though this cottage were apart.

She led him through the living room and out to a tiny flagstoned terrace. There he found Perkinson in a chaise longue, wrapped in a plaid blanket. He smiled a crooked smile at Lovell.

There was a great scar on the left side of his head above the ear and through his pale tonsure, blond once, gray now.

Delicately he took a rubber handball from his right hand with his left, and offered the hand carefully to Lovell.

His speech was slurred but improved and easily understood.

"Sherry, tea, or coffee?" he asked. "We're approaching the high point of my day."

"What are you having?" Lovell asked.

"Sherry. Two glasses. After dinner, two port."

His wife returned with a crystal decanter and two glasses and poured for both.

Perkinson raised his with care, his mouth pursing.

"Thank you, Alice," he said, and watched her leave.

"Half an hour, please, Mr. Lovell," she said, and left them.

"How are you?" Lovell asked.

"Unco-ordinated. They tell me that bit by bit I'll get back. They're really not concerned about minor dysfunction. Funny. I always was.

"I take a glass of sherry and my lips purse while it's still two feet away. I'm clumsy and I don't have much depth perception. Everything I do is a little bit off in time or space or sound. And my thinking is strange. Gaps. I'll be reading *Nicholas Nickleby*—old and familiar—easily, running along half from memory, and then I drop a whole paragraph and can't find it, even if I reread the whole page word by word.

"And developing a thesis or a pattern of thought is just not possible."

"I'm sorry," Lovell said.

Perkinson shook his head and set the glass down more firmly than necessary, the last inches accomplished one by one. He turned to look at it twice where it stood.

"Not your fault."

"Do you think we acted properly?"

Perkinson frowned.

"Properly. Properly. I can't say. I don't remember anything, except the night and looking up at that sail. I remember watching all those lines and the strain on them.

"For the rest, they had a primary responsibility to do what we set out to do. They did that, I have been told. You went with them."

Lovell nodded.

"Did Bartlett give you the statement I made?"

"Yes. I saw Bartlett in Washington. Washington. Walter Reed."

Lovell leaned forward, in anxiety, to draw him closer to what had occurred. But he turned away to his glass again, sipped from it, and replaced it. He closed his eyes for long moments and tipped his head, listening.

"When I gave him my statement, my report," Lovell said with exaggerated calm as his half hour fled, "he was inferring that Amat had or could have deliberately undermined your operation."

Perkinson was suddenly alert, as though he had returned from another place and was anxious to conceal it.

"Did he say 'undermined'? Was that the term he used?"

"No." Lovell shook his head definitely. "But that's what he implied."

"We were all so frustrated. Amat. Madden. Me. I had had enough. I wanted to be free of it all. Let there be an end to it finally. Madden chafing endlessly. No matter how efficient he was and how dedicated and how prepared, there was always something that escaped him and his care.

"That woman you brought to Virginia with you."

He smiled, embarrassedly, and shook his head.

"So typical." He closed his eyes again but continued to speak.

"Amat knew more than Madden. But he had a kitchen approach to what he did. He knew where all the roaches are, he heard all the details, all the gossip, saw all the dirty tablecloths with the diagrams.

"Couldn't categorize anything. Couldn't see behavior as standard, anywhere and everywhere. Too much of a Malay for that. A proud and progressive man.

"He made contact. He can come back when he likes. They'll put him on a desk for a while and then out in the field again marked 'sensitive.' That isn't written down. It's understood. He will count ships from a shore station in one of the Trucial States. Or do analysis of Igorot attitudes.

"It was so much better years ago. When they were informants and we paid them forty dollars a month. When we left they took their money and bought a piece of property with it. The relationship had clarity. We didn't involve them in a social system or a philosophy, we paid them for a task, and didn't move them about in a structure they could never come to terms with."

He laughed explosively.

"We suppress nationalism, race pride; all anathematic to us. One of our obligations to our achievements—to our victories as we lead the world toward Nirvana. But they won't be led by us any more than they could be led by the Macedonians or the Romans or the French or the Germans.

"What have we got to show them that we know the way?"

Lovell shook his head stubbornly.

"Amat was the only one of us who behaved well. He stayed so that I could get away. And I know that feeling of being alone and outside the palings. He had only his own ability—"

"That's what he was trained for," Perkinson said. "That's how he's supposed to function. A stranger in a strange land. He's a citizen of the world. So many nerve endings that are better than a microphone or a camera at best. And at worst, not only useless but dangerous.

"He's my responsibility. I won't forget him."

Perkinson's wife returned and he forced himself to don his quiet smile.

"Still functioning," he told her. "See?"

"Of course," she said, wrapping him in certainty. If there was any concern for his difficulties she did not betray it to Lovell.

She surrounded Perkinson with her own assurance, as though she possessed a special knowledge of a calm and happy future.

Lovell wished Perkinson well and he nodded cheerfully.

At the door, his wife gave him her hand.

"He looks well, doesn't he?" she said.

"Very," Lovell said. "Much better than I had expected."

"But if you come back," she added hurriedly, "wait a few weeks. Perhaps a month."

"Of course," Lovell said. "I understand."

Back in Provincetown, he parked the car on the street before the house in which they were staying. He turned off the engine and sat there reading the instrument labels, his mind occupied only with the present.

"That is all," he told himself. "That any of us can handle, anyway."

He placed the visit in front of Joyce at dinner that evening, like another course.

He had expected little in the way of comment and she did not disappoint him. She looked into his eyes with much concern and was sympathetic.

"How awful for her," she said with sincerity. "To have him come back like that. And so close to retirement, too.

"Will he get better?"

Lovell shrugged.

"Maybe. Hearty New England stock."

There was no more to be said. There were limits to the numbers of changes one could ring upon a marriage, or indeed any other relationship.

They returned home on Sunday afternoon with some lobsters, a couple of pecks of clams, and some jars of beach-plum jelly. They were not so much for the pleasure of the people at home, but rather as a tangible evidence of accomplishment and an expression of the pleasure found in it.

They might have bought a small pine-needle pillow—Lovell had thought of it for a moment, picked one up and sniffed at it—but it seemed to engender both too much and too little. He did not buy it.

He remained reflective and almost indolent for some weeks.

Then he had a telephone call from the launchman at his club.

As ever, the old captain wasted no time.

Lovell picked up his telephone and the voice said, "Your boat's back."

He cackled loudly.

"Looks like shit," he said. "I put it in your slip down at the marina. But you better get down here and tell me what to do about it."

"Why?" Lovell said. "What's the matter?"

"I got other boats to pump out too," he said happily. "I can't leave the club pump in your bilges and run it twenty-four hours a day. Who's going to pay for the electric? Better get your yard to haul it or plant geraniums in it or something."

"I'll be down tonight," Lovell said.

He telephoned to Colleran and to Max and finally to Iacovino. He had not spoken to them since they had returned from Jamaica. With Max and Frank the conversation was strained but they agreed to meet him at the dock that evening.

Iacovino was another matter.

"Is it for dinner?" he said, and when Lovell told him it wasn't, his voice changed to a kind of soapy sincerity that emphasized his utter lack of interest.

"I'd like to have a beer with you," he said, "but I have to sort out my gear.

"Now listen," he added, "if you're racing this summer, you be sure and ask me to come along. There's a lot worse than you are winning races."

"Sure," Lovell said. "I'll call you."

Lovell arrived before the other two. He stood on the pier above the walk that led down to the marina. There was still enough light from the western sky to pick out details. They were not pleasant.

He could hear the steady thumping of the pump as it cut in and out, a dry gasp from the intake hose, and silence. Then minutes later the motor came to life again and the splashing from the outlet hose foamed behind *Avatar*.

Silently, Colleran and Max appeared. He shook their hands awkwardly and they walked down the gangway together.

*Avatar* had been towed up from New York, perhaps lashed alongside some workboat or other, a pump from the other vessel running all the way.

Her topsides were stained and filthy with grease and rubbings from the tires that had been used as fenders. Her mast lay lashed haphazardly along her length, the halliards, stays, and shrouds in a tangle below the butt. The deck stanchions, where they had been removed to accommodate mast and boom, had worked gouges into the deck.

The washboards for the cabin hatch were gone, pried out with a crowbar by the look of the track. The forehatch gaped uncovered, like the top of an old well.

Below, there was little left of any value. There was the smell of bilge water that had entered, the black line of its height around the whole interior of the hull.

The radio was gone and the depth finder, the compass repeater, the direction finder, most of the dishes, bedding, and table silver.

"Engine's had it too, I guess," Colleran said finally.

"Enough to make you puke," Max said. "Every son of a bitch along the way helped himself. They even took the goddamn peanut butter."

Colleran came out of the head.

"Well," he said, "shut off the pump. The intake valve in the head was open. That's where the water came from."

"I thought the hull was sprung," Lovell said. "I thought they dropped it."

Colleran turned the wheel idly. It ran free.

"I think they did that too; feels like the rudder's gone."

"You two want to buy a boat?" Lovell said. "I'll give you a real good price."

He looked at Max and rubbed two fingers together in an age-old gesture.

"What I paid for it originally."

"What are you taking it out on me for!" Max said in a fury. "I didn't do it to you. You did it to yourself. You dug the grave."

Lovell grinned at him.

"Just trying to pass it along. You're closest.

"I'm going back inside the structure. Where the dreams are separate from the reality and stay that way. Yearning is better."

"I don't want to disappoint you," Max said bitterly. "I'll give you twenty-five per cent less than you want. Myself. I don't want any partners."

"Shit," Colleran said. "Cut it out, Max. He's in a bad way."

"Not so bad," Lovell told him.

"Then let him break down," Max said. "Let him cry. Let him ask for help. If he won't ask, let him climb the walls.

"I'm tired of watching him and everybody else manage themselves.

"Fuck him. The inadequate bastard."

Colleran grinned.

"We can't," he said. "That's too much of a luxury for us. We have to put Humpty Dumpty together for our own sakes. We're part of him and what he's done.

"I can show you this, Max, step by step. Listen."

"Don't you do it. Let him."

"He can't, Max. But he trusts us to help. That's why he's sitting there dumb. He's a product of his time. He knows he can't step this mast himself, right? But if he were trying, he'd know he could count on us.

"Just so, he can't tell us what he's feeling now. He can't cry because he doesn't know when to. But he wants us to give him our loyalty and friendship and with no guarantee that he'll ever reciprocate. He's got a low opinion of himself. That low. But we accept, because we know what we are too."

"Great reasoning," Max said dryly.

"He didn't con us," Colleran said. "He pushed us to the wall, in fact. Me too. But so what? His meaning is clear. He's an impersonal man and can't speak of the unspeakable. Weakness and fear and inability to cope, unless you corner him drunk or put him in a padded room. And the minute he comes out of shock he puts on the armor again. And you're faced with this shaved and sensible dummy. But we have a duty to him anyhow."

"I have enough kiddies," Max said. "I'm not Catholic. That's your thing. And I have enough trouble being a shaved and sensible dummy myself. I tried not to, but my nose or my clothes always get in the way."

Lovell listened, pleased. When Colleran struck upon something that was less than peripheral he came to the point of speech himself—to agreement and the desire to expand upon it.

Then it faded to a hum of overheard conversation, the general import clear to him and satisfying, as Max gave ground, not so much to the argument as to his own decency.

He stood up suddenly.

"Come up to the bar," he said. "I want to buy you a drink. You can't leave me alone now."

He led the way.

The bar was almost empty this weekday evening, the cocktail hour was over, the diners at their tables.

There were half a dozen younger men seated about one table. They behaved as though conceived, birthed, and reared there in this room that was designed to look like a sailor's snug a hundred years ago.

They ordered from Eddie, who was both the bartender and waiter at this hour. Eddie's personality had almost disappeared beneath the recollection of all that he had seen and heard over thirty years of service here.

There was an air of apprehension about Eddie, not for himself, but for those he served. As though aware that the prescribed behavior standards that were supposed to prevail there could not be maintained much longer.

When Eddie had served them, they touched glasses solemnly before they drank.

The conversation at the other table was carried on in undertones but punctuated by an occasional sharp exclamation and heads shaken in sadness and disbelief.

Lovell signaled to Eddie.

"I wonder if you'd do me a favor, Eddie," he said quietly. "Ask Mr. Lillis if he'd mind coming over here for a moment. I'd like to speak to him."

He did not turn to watch the colloquy, but Frank did with elaborate pretext.

"He's agreeing," he said quietly. "Said something to his friends about being able to swim."

"Little prick," Max said.

"Little is the last thing he is. He's bigger than Iacovino."

"His muscles are unformed yet," Lovell said, bursting with laughter.

"He's still immature."

"If it comes to that," Colleran said, "let's have a fair fight, John. Kipling says, 'you 'old 'is 'ands and I'll kick 'im.' "

Then he was standing just opposite Lovell's chair.

"Did you want to speak to me?" he said. There was a certain reserve, a coolness to him, a poised confidence. Lovell tried to remember whether he himself had ever possessed it.

He rose and offered his hand and Lillis hesitated a moment and then grasped it momentarily. He introduced Colleran and Max and they nodded, but did not rise. Nor did they offer their hands.

"Drink?"

"Beer."

Eddie brought it, withdrew quickly to the side of the bar, and fixed a stare upon the full-rigged model of a tea clipper on the wall over the door.

Lillis drank half of it in a single pull and sat back in his chair with his arms folded, waiting.

Lovell looked at him directly, presenting himself as equal to equal, yet aware of the imposture. His voice and manner were gilt.

"About the crew of my boat," he said steadily. "One got a fractured skull when a spinnaker fitting on the mast cracked. The other two were not lost. So the story you are telling is not true and it's damaging to me and to Max and Frank, who were also on board."

He gestured at them in their business suits as though their appearance alone were truth.

"That's what I heard down there," Lillis said. "One of my mates heard it from a member of the race committee. They did say they'd never accept another entry from you, and that probably nobody else would either."

"Well," Lovell told him, frowning, "it just isn't true."

"Is that all you wanted to say, sir?" Lillis said, rising.

"I don't have any particular reason to tell the story again, but I do know that when your boat was moored there were only three people on it. Isn't that so?"

Lovell nodded.

"But it's not the whole story. The rest of us were picked up by a patrol boat and flown out to a hospital so the injured man could be treated."

"Right," Lillis said. "I'm sorry I said anything. I apologize if I said anything that hurt you."

"I accept," Lovell muttered. Then Lillis was back across the room. There were smiles and some smothered laughter before they drifted out.

"You should have asked him to crew with us this summer," Max said. "Maybe then he would have changed color a little. Knowing he was in a drowning party."

Colleran drank his drink and held up the empty to Eddie's staring eye.

"If it weren't for us," he said, "Lillis and his friends would have to invent us. So they could have something not to behave like. If we weren't here for horrible examples, how could virtue like his ever appear?"

Lovell nodded thoughtfully and smiled. But Max could not understand.

"Be direct for a change," he said. "I'm tired of being dipped in shit. I'm as good as he is."

"Never," Colleran said. "Never. You're a flawed man. All those adjustments you made weakened you. Sapped your strength. Compromise in one place, you do it in another.

"He didn't believe John. For a minute. I was there on board and I didn't believe John myself.

"But I'm glad we met him. I like to see young men with an oversupply of morality and the willingness to set standards that nobody can measure up to. You have to see that gleam someplace."

"Has to do," Lovell said idly, "with the process of non-aging. The past glows so bright, it's distracting. Turned out to be a lonely place. Full of gratifications at first. Now full of bitterness."

They listened to him and commented from time to time. Later, Eddie brought them roast beef sandwiches and hot mustard.

Max slathered it on and his eyes watered.

They drank brandy afterward. At eleven, when the place was completely empty, they went outside, remembering little of what they had said but conscious of the geometrical figure that they had arranged that would hold them together through time.

The sky was clear and bright and a fingernail of moon was still high.

"Come on," Lovell said grandly. "Let's take her out and sink her."

"Fine idea. Fine, fine," Max said. They sat down on the steps and looked out at the harbor buoy. There was a good breeze tonight, still cold, from the northeast. The tide was on the flood with the wind and the fresh salt tang was heavy upon it.

"Negative," Colleran said. "We all deserve better than that. The boat, the people, the sport. Proper served," he corrected himself carefully. "More proper served by raising the ensign again. Going to sea again."

"Under another name?" Max asked. "*Dauntless?*"

"Same name," Colleran said. "Same crew."

"We could put a little plaque in the cabin," Lovell suggested.

"I accept that," Colleran said, considering, with thumb and forefinger pulling at his lower lip.

"Gentlemen," he said, raising the brandy glass he had brought out with him:

"To resurgence."

Each of them sipped ceremoniously and Colleran walked

around to the chimney and flung the glass against it. They looked at the shards lying in the grass, and more: themselves sailing in this night breeze, comfortable in the cockpit in their heavy sweaters, the bow lifting to these low crests, apart but dependent upon each other.

That warmed them and pleased them so that, satisfied, they could part.